FATEFUL WATERS

FATEFUL WATERS

TROUBLES IN LOVE-LAND BOOK ONE

J. M. ANTON

Half Appy Press

Published by Half Appy Press

ISBN: 978-0-9962645-0-1

Typesetting services by bookow.com

Acknowledgments

Thank you to my frontline editors and proofreaders Pat and Kellie Anton. Also thanks to Kellie for editing the German language inclusions.

I also want to thank my pre-publication readers for their support and evaluations of the original release of Fateful Waters in 2012: Sandy S, Mary Lou Lazor, Joan Adamak, and Reynold Bowen.

Front cover design by Goddess Fish.

The 2015 edition of Fateful Waters as the first book in the" Troubles in Love-Land" Series was edited by consulting editors at Another Set of Eyes

CONTENTS

CHAPTER 1

ALEXANDRA, reluctantly, started on the trip to Decker's place on a bright sunny afternoon. An hour north of Lubbock, the sun had gone into hiding behind some ominous black clouds. She felt the same sense of foreboding that she had experienced upon her first encounter with David Decker. She and Melinda had barely checked into their shared suite when David appeared out of the blue. She knew that Melinda must have told him of their impending arrival. Lexie made the first designated turn on her route, piloting Melinda's graduation gift onto a gravel road. The Escalade bit into the gravel and traveled the mile and a quarter without incident. Her written instructions and the GPS were in agreement, so far. Another half-hour and she came to fork where she turned left onto a rutted dirt road, and that was when it started to rain. She slipped the large SUV into four-wheel drive and turned the wipers on low. All that accomplished was to make a mess of the accumulated dust on the windshield, but several squirts of the washer fluid cleared a small spot for her to see where she was going.

Her mood was as dark as the clouds that had taken over a previously bright blue sky. Texas hadn't looked much different to her when she exited the interstate upon their arrival, but she had been feeling ill and not paying much attention. Scenery blurred by at seventy miles an hour as they had traveled the homogenous interstate system that offered the same fast food joints, chain restaurants, and box stores from coast to coast. Lexie had opted to drive most of the trip. It was easier for her to control bouts of carsickness when she was in control of the vehicle and was required to concentrate on traffic. She'd only vaguely taken notice of the absence of green as they entered Oklahoma with its endless fields of grasshopper-like oil pumping rigs. Her perception of the Texas panhandle underwent a drastic change once she left the relative safety of the Lubbock hotel parking lot to join Melinda and her heartthrob for dinner.

She applied the breaks at another fork in the road that was not on the instructions, or the GPS. "So much for backup!" She grumbled. The SUV skidded in the slime covering the previously dusty road. Lexie retrieved her phone from an inside pocket of her navy handbag. Disgusted, she laid it on the center console. Smart or not, the directional phone apps had not shed any light on her dilemma. She was really beginning to feel ill, so she twisted of the cap on the antibiotic that she had just picked up at the drugstore. The prescription label said it was to be taken with food, but she was desperate to head of a recurrence of what sure felt like the flu. She downed the pill with the remainder of a bottle of water she'd placed in the cup holder. Lexie picked up the small communication device, located Melinda's name, and she poked the small screen much harder than required to connect to her friend. She wanted to scream! Why me Lord?

Melinda didn't have a clue how to direct her. Lexie slipped into her navy jacket while her friend checked with David. As the rain increased, the heat of earlier began to cool and she was experiencing a chill. Lexie switched from the air conditioner to the heater.

She was sitting in the middle of a dirt road, in an increasing rain, and the surface was quickly becoming a quagmire. She hoped that

Melinda was writing down directions, and that was why she was taking so much time.

Roommates since their freshman year at Ohio State, Alexandra Parker and Melinda Potter had become close friends. After nearly five years, their friendship had grown to the point they were familiar with the other's personality quirks. Lexie knew Melinda well enough to be skeptical about the accuracy of the written directions her friend had left for her when she went on ahead with David. Commonsense had dictated that she enter his ranch address in the GPS, just in case.

Finally, Melinda was back on the phone and in the nick of time. Lexie felt the Cadillac sinking into the softening road surface while she had been waiting for further directions.

"Lexie? David says to take the left fork. He says that you are only about a mile from the house."

"A mile in this stuff might just as well be a hundred."

"Quit complaining, Lexie, all you have to do is put the Escalade in four-wheel drive and you will be okay. See you in a bit.

Lexie didn't answer her. Instead, she merely threw her phone on the console.Aggravated with herself for agreeing to this trip, she rolled the vehicle forward. Mud flew and the SUV fishtailed a little, but the tires found purchase. Less than a quarter of a mile crawled by until the road suddenly disappeared into a roaring creek. With nowhere to turn around, she began backing over her tracks. Progress was slow. The small single wiper on the rear window made it difficult to navigate through the increasing downpour. She could hear Melinda's voice in her mind "David says, David says". She gave herself a mental shake and concentrated on reverse driving.

Back out on the dirt road, she made a decision to take the right fork. Assuming her mind was functioning past her blinding headache, she recalled that back the way she had come the same previously dry creek that flooded the left fork also ran under a culvert on the main dirt excuse for a road. It was probably washed out by this time too. The right fork rose on a very slight incline and promised higher ground. She was thinking the higher terrain could keep her from drowning, but the mud was getting deeper. Lexie was worried about getting bogged down in the middle of nowhere. Most likely any help she may be able summon from her friend would never be able to reach her in time to help. She was on her own. She had the wipers up full force and was driving slower to avoid sliding off the edge of the slick surface. The right fork spilt again about a mile from the last divide. Once more, she picked the option with the potential for higher elevation. She proceeded at a snail's pace with her vehicle in low gear as she squinted through the windshield into the growing monsoon. She rounded a curve in the road, and a large shadow suddenly loomed in front of her. It occupied the center of the road. Lexie swerved to avoid what appeared to be a large animal and slid smack into the muck at the right side of the road.

She felt the Escalade sink. Her temper broke the tenuous hold she had on it. She turned off the engine and barreled out the driver's side door. So intent on venting her frustration on the huge cow that blocked the road, she forgot that she wearing her navy dress pumps. The cow was the recipient of the frustration she couldn't vent on Melinda and her creepy Romeo. David Decker was attractive enough physically with his black wavy hair, cornflower blue eyes, and engaging smile, but there was something sinister about the man. Lexie sank in six inches of muck and with the next step her shoes were buried in it.

"Are you in a hurry to be hamburger? I could have run you over in this blinding rain! Now, look, you've killed the damned Cadillac."

The beast wouldn't move out of the road. Pushing on its rump didn't accomplish anything, nor did smacking it on the hip. That little bout of temper left her with a stinging hand. The white face was halterless—"it's not a horse," she reminded herself—and she didn't have a rope or even a belt. Lexie was nearly knee-deep in slop. She stood there glaring at the cow with her hands planted on her hips.

The huge cow let out a bellow while she was assessing the situation. A small echo bounced back from a few feet away. Lexie spotted a small calf stuck in a mud pit. The only parts visible were the head and a small portion of its back. The little one was sinking in a run-off of muck that had flowed from slightly higher terrain behind it. At that moment, the no rope or belt issue was a real dilemma. Lexie improvised and removed her navy jacket that matched her already trashed slacks. She waded closer to the calf and hoped she wouldn't sink along with it. She kept a wary eye on its watchful mother as she slipped her jacket around the calf's neck and gave a tug. She managed to raise its head a little higher, but it was stuck and couldn't get any traction to assist in its rescue attempt. Giving a little stronger tug she lost her own traction and ended up sitting on her butt in the mud while propping up the small creature's head. Lexie was in immediate danger of sinking in the muck along with the baby cow when the ghost riders appeared from out of the storm.

One minute, no one was around for miles, and then—poof—there they were. Maybe I'm hallucinating? Flitted through her mind. She was trying hard to focus, but her head was throbbing. Lexie was beginning to shake uncontrollably. Through the veil of rain, one rider appeared a normal person as they rode closer. He sat astride a sorrel-colored cowpony with a white star, but that was about all she could tell. From the belly down both horses were thick with mud that had splashed up on the animals, and their riders' legs were in much the same condition. Both horsemen wore black Stetsons and outback-type oilskin dusters. The dark cowboy was bigger than the other man and was mounted on a large black stallion. It was he who brought forth the image of a ghost rider.

"You need some help, little girl?"

His voice was a low baritone, close to a bass, with a thick Texan drawl. She was feeling a bit weak from her trek through the mud and trying to free the calf. It was hard to decipher his words through the roaring in her ears and unrelenting rain. He repeated the question as he rode closer and dismounted.

All she could say was, "He is drowning in the mud."

Without another word the dark rider caught a loop from the other cowboy's rope and replaced her jacket with the rope before he picked her up out of the mud. He unceremoniously deposited her by the side of her vehicle while he returned to the hapless calf. Gratefully, she leaned against the bogged-down Cadillac for support. Her head was beginning to swim, and a bone-shattering chill had over taken her, but Lexie realized she was no longer shivering as she had been sitting in the run off with the newborn calf. This can't be good, she thought. Maybe my body is shutting down? She watched the tall cowboy wade into the mud hole and lift the backend of the calf while the rider on the sorrel backed his horse giving a steady tug on the rope. Momma cow and baby were on higher ground in no time and wandering back to their herd.

Her mind registered that she was way overdue for her dinner invitation. She reached in through the still open door for her phone. It was time to call Melinda and tell her friend to have dinner without her. The phone had fallen to the floor near the gas pedal when she swerved ditching the expensive SUV. Lexie leaned in to retrieve it smearing mud on the light gray leather interior. Once she latched on to it and righted herself into the driver side bucket seat, her efforts to manipulate the small phone with her muddy hands sent it right through her grip. She gasped in disbelief as her iPhone took a dive out the open door sinking into the muck. "That's the last straw! I knew I should have just stayed in Lubbock," she grumbled to the fast disappearing phone. It was now buried in the same muddy grave as her navy pumps.

"This is just terrific! I am supposed to be the stabilizing influence according to Melinda's parents", she grumbled. It was Melinda's parents who had convinced her that she needed a break after the stress of finals. Mrs. Potter insisted that Lexie needed a rest to spring back from her run-down condition following a nasty bout of the flu, and Lexie's mother had agreed with Linda Potter.

Lexie'd been aware of the steamy e-mails Mel was sending to David Decker in response to his romantic crock of bull transmissions. What she hadn't known was that Melinda was planning on traveling to Texas after graduation to meet her Internet match service's most recent compatible male.

Lexie was losing her tenuous hold on reality as she slid down into the mud against the side of the muck covered, once white, Escalade and gave up the search for her phone and shoes. Sitting in the mud was the last thing that she remembered clearly until she woke up in a hospital where everyone was calling her Mrs. Ross.

******

Most of the herd was up closer to the ranch out of harm's way for the moment, and the men had been rounding up the inevitable strays when the forecasted rains hit. Remnants of tropical storms seldom made it this far north, but when they did flash floods were inevitable. All the cattle were accounted for except the big Hereford cow ready to drop a late calf. They'd left the other hands to move the rounded up strays toward the relative safety of the ranch. Cutter, the owner of the outfit, and Jim Rodriguez, his foreman, went in search of the old cow. They had a hunch where she would be, and under most circumstances it wouldn't have worried them. She liked to drop her calves down near the water, but today it could prove deadly if she sought an isolated spot near there to deliver.

Cutter was exhausted, having only returned late that morning, from four days in Dallas. He'd not yet unpacked when he joined the rest of his crew to move the cattle away from potential flash flood areas.

Riding in the midst of a torrential downpour and several inches of mud made for slow progress. The river was emitting an earsplitting roar by the time they approached the spot where they figured the expectant cow would seek solitude. A larger object entered Cutter's peripheral as they continued to scan the surroundings for their missing bovine. Jim saw it about the same time and let loose with a string of cuss words that sizzled out into another cloudburst. A large, mostly mud colored, vehicle was rounding the curve and about to run down his pregnant Hereford. Too far away to holler a warning they waited for the inevitable collision. Then the driver swerved at the last moment and sunk that fancy rig to its rocker panels.

Some days it paid unexpected dividends to battle the elements. Neither he nor Jim would ever forget watching the driver, dressed like one of those professional women on TV, exit her SUV as if ready for a fight. The little woman rounded on Mamma cow. She was hollering at it and giving it a piece of her mind while trying to push it out of the road. She even smacked the cow on the rump. Mamma cow let out a threat of her own, and the little lady backed off. No. Cutter thought, it wasn't the cow's threat that stopped the irate driver's assault, but something else that had caught her attention. Both cattlemen knew what distracted her was most likely a newborn calf. The men saw her pull off her jacket to wrap it around the calf's neck as they rode closer. At that point, she either sat or fell down beside it. She remained there propping that small head above the mud and sinking along with it!

The mud-covered woman stared at him as if he were the headless horseman. He had to ask her twice if she needed some help. With Jim's rope securely around the small critter to keep its head above the mud hole, he plucked the calf's would-be rescuer out of the deepening mud hole and set her on her feet by her Cadillac. Then he went back to help Jim haul the newborn out of the mud. Jim took the calf up across his lap and rode a safe distance from the rising water before releasing it. The calf was none the worse for its experience, largely due to the little lady keeping its head elevated. Cutter turned around to check on her and was amazed to see her sitting with her back propped against the side of her mud-splattered ride. She continued looking at him like he was the devil incarnate. He approached her slowly. Her up swept hairdo was falling down on one side. Soaking wet and covered in mud, he would be surprised if she weighed a hundred pounds. The continuing down pour had rinsed the heavy mud from her soaked once white silk blouse. It clung to her petite form affording an enticing peek at a lacy bra that barely hid her pert breasts. She was obviously chilled; her nipples were puckered and erect. Cutter needed to get a grip and stop ogling the stranded little woman with the mistrustful blue eyes.

He took precious moments to walk around the vehicle as far as possible and wipe off the front license plate that declared the Cadillac was from Ohio. Curiosity took hold, "Are you lost?"

"What makes you think I am lost, cowboy?"

Her voice was an octave above a whisper, shaky and thin, but she definitely had a Yankee accent. He tried again, "My name is Cutter. What's your name?" She looked at him as if he were speaking a foreign language.

"I lost it."

"You lost your name?" She wasn't making any sense.

"Of course not. I lost my shoes, and my phone, not to mention a mangy cow killed my car, but I haven't lost my name."

She spoke to him as if he were a little slow on the uptake. Okay, I will give it one more try, he thought.

"My name is Alexandra," she volunteered, before he could ask again. It was obvious she didn't trust him. He figured it could be she had caught him scrutinizing her physical attributes. Cutter tried to be patient with her, but the nearby stream was quickly becoming a raging torrent, and he couldn't let her stay where she was.

"Alexandra, we need to move away from here, or we're both going to drown."

She shook her head staring at his big black stallion with huge terrified eyes when he suggested that she mount his horse to ride out of there with him. He took the decision out of her hands. The rising water was lapping at the right side of the Cadillac and they were out of time. Cutter plucked her out of the mud, once more, and carried her over to deposit her on his saddle. She had the presence of mind to straddle it. He quickly mounted behind her, and spurred Rowdy to higher ground. Her silk blouse clung to her small frame and she shivered uncontrollably. Opening his duster, he pulled her close to him and closed the front over her. She objected at first, but then relented out of concern for Rowdy when Cutter scolded her, "Quit wiggling. You're making it harder for my horse to pick his way through this muck." She settled down immediately. He'd expected her to be cold when he pulled her against his chest and had been worried about hyperthermia. Of even more concern was the fact that she was burning up and becoming lethargic. He figured it would probably be a good idea to get her to focus by talking to him.

"Alexandra? I'll bet that they call you Alex." Her voice was fading and becoming weaker, but she responded.

"Wrong. My friends call me Lexie. However, you can call me Alexandra."

He suppressed the urge to laugh. He had a hunch under normal circumstances she was a handful. "What were you doing out here Alexandra?"

"Playing in the mud with your cows. They are your cows, aren't they?"

"Yep, they're mine. You like cows, Alexandra?"

"I like them just fine, served up as a medium rare porterhouse."

Her response surprised Cutter given the effort she had put forth to save the calf, and he told her so. "You must really like steak to jump in the mud with a potential dinner."

"Well…it's only a baby. You really ought to make hamburger out of that cow, once the baby is weaned."

"You don't think she would make good steaks?"

"She doesn't deserve to be steaks. She's a crappy mother, parking her baby in the middle of a road. It's like a human telling their kids to go play in traffic!"

He was not going to laugh at her or set her straight about cattle tonight, but it was a strain to keep the laughter from becoming audible. Thankfully, the house was in sight, and Jim had already alerted Maria who was ready to take over the care of their unexpected guest. Alexandra was barely lucid, but he knew Maria would be able to handle the situation. He left her in his longtime cook and housekeeper's care. "Maria, this is Alexandra." Then he was back out the door to take care of his exhausted horse.

Maria was amazed that the small girl hadn't slid through Cutter's hold, like a slippery little fish when he deposited her in the mudroom off the kitchen. Maria automatically guided her shivering charge to the adjacent room that housed a small tub and shower stall. She didn't like the way Alexandra looked. The girl could not seem to communicate and could barely stand on her own. A shower was out of the question, so Maria opted to use the tub.

Once the mud was washed off in the warm bath, their houseguest stopped shaking like a leaf in an early winter snowstorm. It was obvious to Maria as she assisted the slightly built blonde from the tub that none of her own clothes would work for Alexandra. She estimated they were approximately the same height of five foot and three or four inches, but that was it. Clothes intended for Maria's ample bosom and rounded physique would wrap around this slim girl twice or fall off completely. Only her tall wool socks fit, but her charge would most likely expire from shock if she got a glimpse of herself Cutter's housekeeper made her character assessment based on the expensive, fashionable, clothes that the girl had been wearing when she arrived. Maria didn't think the young woman's clothing was salvageable. The best Maria was able to do was fetch one of Cutter's flannel shirts. At least the blue plaid covered Alexandra to her knees, and Maria was able to roll up the long sleeves on the girls limp arms. The girl was barely conscious. Maria set the tea to brew, and then was able to coax Cutter's foundling to accept an oral thermometer. Cutter was always carting home strays or injured animals when they were children, but this was no abandoned puppy. He had really outdone himself this time. Maria retrieved the thermometer as she placed the cup of tea in front of Alexandra, who was slumping in her chair and listing a bit. Maria kept a close eye on the young woman while she read the results. Aone hundred and four readout!

Maria punched in the number for Doctor Joe while her charge sipped tea. The housekeeper summoned the doctor, and then she contacted her husband Jim. His cell only rang twice.

"I need you, Jim. This girl is really sick. She's running an extremely high temperature. You or Cutter will have to carry her to the other end of the house and put her to bed until doctor Joe gets here."

Maria had a premonition that this rescue was going to backfire on all of them.

CHAPTER 2

MELINDA was starting to worry. What was keeping Lexie? She should have arrived over an hour ago, and Mel was unable to reach her. Calls to her friend's phone consistently rolled over to voice mail. A chill accompanied by a sense of foreboding began to penetrate her bones despite the cozy warmth of the blazing log fireplace. She knew that Lexie hadn't fully recovered from the miserable bout of flu that had circulated around campus toward the end of March. It had irritated Mel that her parents had sent Lexie along as a moderating influence. Money talks, and her parents had only footed the bill for the trip as long as her roommate accompanied her. Melinda began to resent her friend because of her parents' interference. She tried to quell her ire by counting her blessings that her father hadn't insisted on sending his bodyguard along, too. The call to invite Lexie for dinner with her and David hadn't gone well. . Her mind replayed their conversation earlier in the day.

"Melinda, I really don't feel like traveling to God knows where to have dinner."

"You have to eat, so why not have dinner with us?" Mel had argued.

"I think David has a more intimate dinner for two planned."

"Don't be silly. He wants you to join us."

"I doubt that. I think I will hit the Outback Steak place, then call it an early night."

"The least you could do, Lexie, is give him a chance. Have dinner with us, and then you can report back that he isn't some kind of an ogre." Okay, that had come out rather snippy she admitted to herself.

"So, give me the damn directions." Lexie had sounded really annoyed and put-upon about the dinner coercion tactic. Her friend had a sixth sense about people that was extremely annoying. She'd disliked David from the beginning. Melinda had shrugged of her friend's concerns. After all, it was just a feeling, she'd thought. She'd also reasoned that Lexie didn't have a man in her own life, and her objections to David were probably jealousy. Curious she'd inquired, "Haven't you ever been wrong about a negative first impression, Lexie?"

"Rarely." Had been her friend's cryptic reply.

The last she'd spoken with her traveling companion, Lexie had been lost at a crossroad. She'd been caught in the beginning of an epic rainstorm about a mile from the ranch house, and she'd sounded really peeved. Melinda wished she could be as relaxed and confident as David that Lexie had gone back to the hotel, which was their short-term home. But she wasn't back at the hotel suite yet, and she was not answering her phone. Melinda smiled at David, accepting the offered glass of red wine and hoped it would take the edge off the guilt trip that was threatening to overwhelm her.

******

Melinda didn't have a clue what time it was when she woke, but the unremitting sun was burning through her still-closed eyelids like surgeon's laser scalpel. She couldn't decide what hurt the most her eyes or the ceaseless pounding in her head. As she gingerly opened her eyes it became apparent as the room stopped spinning that she had never made it back to the hotel. She thought it strange that she didn't recall drinking much, but events of the prior evening after dinner escaped her. A panicked thought galvanized her. Oh my God! Lexie!

Her stomach pitched, joining the rest of her rebelling body as she put her feet on the floor and attempted to rise. She located her Blackberry and tried to reach her friend, but the message declared her out of the area. No answer at their hotel room number either. She fought rising nausea while she waited for the irritated manager to check on their room. An optimistic thought took hold in her slowly clearing mind — Maybe Lexie was asleep and had her phone turned off? She paced impatiently for the manager to report back to her.

"No, Señorita. The room is empty."

"Are you sure?"

"Si, the beds have not been used since the maids cleaned the room this morning."

Now what to do? She wondered. David was conspicuously absent. The thought of a shower beckoned to her, and the warm spray relieved some of the aches that plagued her body. She felt foul. It was obvious she and David had engaged in some rowdy sex, but she couldn't remember any of it! Melinda, as was her habit, took inventory of her reflection as she wiped the steamy mirror over the bathroom washbasin. She towel dried her dark brown, nearly black, locks and assessed her new spiral perm. Her face was more round than heart shaped like Lexie's flawless face. Melinda squinted at her reflection through her thick lashed blurry brown eyes. She was relieved that no annoying acne blemishes had shown up to mar her complexion. She cupped her tender breasts assessing her bosom and taking pride in her ability to fill a D bra cup. Her absent friend was merely a B, at best. Melinda's estimate of her hour glass figure reassured her that David's interest was in her as a beautiful woman, and had absolutely zero to do with her parents' wealth.

A rumbling in the pit of her stomach hollered, "Feed me!" She found a note on the fridge while scrounging around the kitchen for sustenance. It read, Melinda, Gone to check on storm damage. I will also check near the fork for your SUV. Love, D.D.

Melinda finished up her toast, orange slices, and a mug of stale coffee that she'd warmed in a battered microwave. She decided to make one more attempt to connect with her friend. Still no response, but she left one more message.

She located the proper law enforcement for the outlying area north of Lubbock and punched in the number. The next voice she heard was the heavily accented drawl of the sheriff's dispatcher. Tears ran freely as she explained about her missing friend. Time passed slowly, and it seemed like hours passed while she waited for the sheriff to arrive. Finally, she heard a knock on the door.

"About time you got here!" She let her frustration out on the hapless deputy when she yanked open the front door. He'd made the trip out in slightly over an hour while traversing still mud and debris covered roads. To her impatient mind, she'd been pacing David's house for an eternity waiting for the deputy's arrival.

Melinda fought for control, placing her shaking hands in her lap. After relating the events of the evening before, she retrieved another tissue from her handbag to stem the overflowing tears. She listened closely to his questions as he read the notes he'd been scribbling on the small pad that he carried in his shirt pocket. She noticed when he entered the house and removed his western hat that he had dark blond hair almost the color of Lexie's, but cut in a close military style. Deputy Boyd was, she estimated, in his early thirties, slightly over six feet tall, and very well built. Unlike David who had the slender build of a runner, the deputy was heavily muscled with broad shoulders. He sure looked good in his uniform, but his hazel eyes were unnervingly penetrating as he questioned her.

"When did you last hear from your friend?"

"Lexie called me about six thirty yesterday to ask for additional directions."

"And did you give them to her?"

"Not exactly. I'm not familiar with the area or very good at giving directions. David dictated the directions that I left for her at our hotel suite yesterday before coming out here. When she called he gave me directions to adjust her route. David said she was only about a mile from his place."

"Why didn't he talk to her and give her the new information to adjust her route?"

"Lexie doesn't really like David, and he knows it. He tried to talk me out of extending an invitation for her to join us.

"I'll look into this, and let you know if your friend or your vehicle turn up."

"Deputy Boyd, could you drop me off at the hotel in Lubbock? I'm kind of stranded here, and maybe Lexie has returned to our suite by now."

"Where is Decker?"

She bristled at his tone; it was obvious he didn't like David. "He is out looking for Lexie," she lied. Mel immediately realized the lawman knew her response was a fabrication.

Boyd agreed to escort Melinda back to the hotel. There was always the possibility her friend had returned or had left a message. He didn't tell the distraught brunette with the soft doe-like eyes chances were her vehicle and her friend had been swept away in the floodwaters.

He left her in the hotel room after making a systematic search of the suite. The girls were staying in style. He had noted as he surveyed the off white walls of their temporary home with its tan Berber carpet, and green printed window drapes. Both double beds were neatly made, and there wasn't a single wrinkle in the tan spreads. The sitting room, where they had first entered the suite, was decorated with two green upholstered chairs that coordinated with the drapes and flanked a square table with a brass reading lamp that craned its dual neck for the occupant of either chair. The room also held a forty-inch flat screen TV. Everything was immaculate. Melinda's laptop and the landline were the only items that occupied the faux oak desk next to the entry. Miss Parker's laptop had been sitting on top of the dresser in their shared bedroom. The staff had cleaned the girl's bathroom, including the tan and white floor tile. The small kitchenette floor matched the tile in the bath, and it was easy to tell that both had been scrubbed early that morning. Every table, dresser, and cabinet of oak shined like it was freshly polished. The linens and toiletries were fresh and untouched. It was obvious to both of them her friend hadn't been here today. Boyd left instructions for Melinda to stay put so that he could contact her when, and if he found out something.

Melinda fought the urge to squirm under his intense gaze when she made the mistake of mentioning that she no longer had transportation, so it was unlikely she was going anywhere.

"You managed to hitch a ride with Decker yesterday, instead of waiting for your roommate to return with your vehicle. Again, just stay put until you hear from me."

"Who did that man think he was ordering around?" She grumbled to the empty suite while placing her phone on the charging pad. "No one ever talks to me like that and gets away with it!" She ordered room service before she checked her e-mail. Messages popped up from college friends, home, and she had a half-dozen Facebook friend requests, but not a thing from Lexie. Melinda decided to put off notifying her parents or Lexie's mother until the judgmental deputy found her, one way or the other.

CHAPTER 3

Patrick Boyd scanned through the department database looking for reports filed since the flooding the day before. He checked with the Rangers, fire rescue, Lubbock police, and the National Guard command assigned to the cleanup and rescue effort. Things were moving frustratingly slow with the sheriff's office operating on a generator. Most power and landlines were still out. He was left with radio units that didn't connect with other agencies and cell towers that were overwhelmed. He had placed an APB on the radio before he left earlier on another of what had become an endless series of calls for help.

Like first responders all over most of the Panhandle and West Texas, Pat was running on adrenaline and pure nerve. It was another two and a half days before Melinda Potter's Cadillac Escalade was located. It turned up more than ten miles from where her friend had last been reported. Written reports were filed along photos showing the crushed remains of the SUV minus the driver's side door. The Cadillac was wedged between two large trees; Melinda's SUV had been snagged by a submerged barbwire fence. Rescuers had to remove a large John Deere from atop the smaller vehicle before they could determine that there was no one to be rescued, or even a body to recover. So, where was Alexandra Parker?

Perhaps she'd gotten out before the SUV was swept away, but she should have turned up by now, unless she had drowned in the raging current and was now buried under mud and storm debris. Her handbag containing her ID was found tangled in the branches of the makeshift dam. Most of the items now carefully spread out before Patrick were soaked and illegible, excluding the laminated Ohio driver's license and a student ID from The Ohio State University. Pat reissued the APB to a wider police net now that the phone lines were back in use. However quite a few of the outlying cell towers were still down. He used the information provided by the license. Melinda's earlier description of her friend as blonde, blue eyed, and about four inches shorter than she was pretty much matched what was on the other woman's driver's license. She had also stated that her friend did not possess as large a bosom as she had. Patrick Boyd swallowed, only to discover that his spit had dried up. As the deputy working on her friend's disappearance, he had been avoiding lingering overlong on Melinda's curvy form. He had pretended to take note of her physical qualities for the first time, and then had made his excuses. Patrick had needed to attend to other matters that had backlogged, but his hasty retreat had more to do with putting space between him and the enticing Miss Potter.

Back at the office, the deputy had been able to add Lexie's height of five foot three plus her weight of a hundred and five to Melinda's description of her friend. He downloaded a larger version of Alexandra's photo from the Ohio Bureau of Motor Vehicles. He then tagged the resulting poster with large bold font "Missing!" for the heading. Her name was added below the photo followed by instructions to call the sheriff's office. He faxed the information to area hospitals and the local media.

Exhausted, he resisted the temptation to call Melinda about the discovery of her car. That approach was too impersonal for the current turn of events. Dread wove its tentacles through a usually stoic persona to the point he had to give himself a mental reprimand. *This isn't the first time you have had to deliver unwanted news. Get a hold of yourself, Boyd!*

Melinda answered the suite door on the second knock. Her hopeful expression changed abruptly to one of belligerence when he chastised her for opening the door before she knew who was on the other side. Patrick realized the young man at the check in desk had called up to alert her that he was on his way up, but it was easier to deal with her a bit hostile than too optimistic.

She held the door wide and made a sweeping motion with her free hand while inviting him in. Dripping sarcasm, she said. "Deputy Boyd! What an unexpected pleasure. Won't you please come in?"

He settled into the chair in front of the small desk and glanced, out of habit, toward the screen displaying her Facebook activity. She quickly crossed the room and closed the lid on the laptop. He placed the file folder in his possession on top of it. "These photos were taken at the scene where your vehicle was discovered."

Melinda stared in horror at the mangled remains of her new Escalade. Arms wrapped around her midsection as if she were attempting to ward off a sudden chill, she whispered, "Lexie?"

"We haven't been able to locate her yet. Her shoulder bag was found tangled in the branches of a downed tree a few feet from the submerged vehicle."

Tears were running freely, "She wouldn't have left without it."

"She could have done exactly that in a split second choice between life or certain death."

"You think she's still alive?"

"Until her body turns up, we are working on that premise. We've sent a photo and description to all law enforcement. Area hospitals received a faxed bulletin this morning. We had your SUV towed to the city police impound."

Patrick handed her a card with the police impound information on it. "You'll need this information to have your insurance adjuster look at it."

After he departed, Melinda decided to put off calling the insurance company for a few days. Before she could contact the adjuster, she would have to inform her parents about the loss of the Cadillac. She wanted to wait in hopes that her friend would materialize soon alive. Then she wouldn't have to tell her parents and Lexie's mother of her loss, too.

CHAPTER 4

LEXIE's head throbbed in time with an annoying incessant beeping sound, like a smoke alarm nagging her to change its battery. The air had a strange odor or lack of. She tried to open her eyes and get her bearings, but her lids were like lead jackets refusing to budge. The effort was exhausting. She sank back into the restful, silent, dark void.

Strange voices battled with the odd mechanical sounds the next time she surfaced from the seemingly endless abyss. She vaguely recalled the beep–beep–beep sound as the fog lifted. This time, she also heard a strange raspy breathing that brought images of Darth Vader to her mind. A high-pitched female voice with a childlike quality fit right in with the rest of the bizarre sounds. The male tenor in the conversation reverberated in her skull, but neither of the voices were familiar. They were discussing someone named Ross, and it appeared she was knocking at death's door. Her husband was spending so much time at her side that the hospital administration was considering charging double for the room. She found it difficult to process the information inundating her. Again, she tried to open her eyes; they fluttered a little, but remained glued shut.

A heavyset, middle-aged nurse was bent over Lexie peering closely at her face.

"How is she?"

"Good evening, Mr. Ross. Her vitals are much better. I swear I just saw her eyelashes flutter. I'll make a note of the time and notify the doctor your wife appears to be attempting to open her eyes."

Cutter pulled the blue vinyl clad chair closer to the bedside, picked up her IV free right hand and leaned a little nearer.

"Come on, Lex, let's make a little more effort here. This Sleeping Beauty routine has gone far enough. You're going to have to do this on your own; Prince Charming isn't going to show up."

Her hand felt warmer, but it had been four long miserable days since Doctor Callahan had her life-flighted to this torture chamber in Amarillo. She looked unbelievably pale and fragile. Her lack of response concerned him; he didn't recall a word from her after declaration that her friends called her Lexie, but he could call her Alexandra. The spirited little woman was hooked up to a machine that breathed for her while IV bags dripped fluids through the tube attached to her bruised left hand, and another tube disappeared under the sheet. She sure wasn't going to be happy about this invasion of her person, if he was any judge of character. She was most likely going to fillet him too when she joined the world again. He sighed, sat back in the chair still holding her hand, and dozed off.

****

On the morning of the fifth day following the flash flood Deputy Boyd made the trip northwest to the Rocking R. A local TV station ran a report on the missing Alexandra Parker. The story included her photo and the contact number for information. Patrick had about given up on locating the girl alive when Maria Rodriguez called the office.

He sat at the kitchen table occasionally taking down notes as Maria related the circumstances that brought Alexandra Parker to Cutter Ross's home. "We didn't know the girl's last name. Cutter was only able to get her first name, Alexandra."

"Where is Alexandra now, Mrs. Rodriguez?"

"She was very sick; Doctor Joe said she had pneumonia. He sent her in a helicopter to a hospital in Amarillo."

"Thanks for reporting her whereabouts. I will advise her friend and family that she has been located and is alive. I'll be in touch."

First thing Patrick did was to try to contact Dr. Joe Callahan to arrange a visit. He left a message with the doctor's answering service. His next order of business was to call Melinda to determine her location and access her state of mind.

Melinda had been working up the courage to call her folks when she got the call from Deputy Boyd. He'd located Lexie, alive! The phone call could wait one more day. David wouldn't be happy she'd procrastinated once more. It was his opinion that she was irresponsible for not dealing with the insurance matter right away. Too damn bad. She wanted to see Lexie first.

******

Lexie swam to the top of the black sea enveloping her toward the bright light. Was it daylight or the light to the afterworld? At this juncture, it didn't matter; she was fed up with existing in her dark purgatory. She broke through the persistent darkness and stared into the face of a gray-haired nurse clad in pale blue scrubs. The nurse's completion turned grayer than her hair, and she quickly exited Lexie's view. It occurred to Lexie that she must look a fright to be able to send a nurse into such a hasty retreat.

She took inventory of her surroundings: machines beeped and buzzed around her. Lexie attempted to move in order to survey more of what appeared to be a hospital room, but was pulled up short by a pain in her left hand. A glance toward the source of the ache revealed a needle was taped to the back of her hand. With her eyes still not fully focused, she traced the attached thin tubing to a pair of clear bags above her head that fed the offending tube. She reached up with a functioning right hand and removed the nasty thing stuck in her nose. Lexie was working on removing the tape from her left hand when the nurse who had just taken flight returned with a doctor in tow. It appeared she had regained her color and her bossy voice.

"Stop that, Mrs. Ross!"

"Who the hell is Mrs. Ross?" Lexie hadn't seen anyone else in the room. She appeared to be the only occupant. A thought flitted through her foggy mind: My medical coverage doesn't include a private room. The next words out of the nurse's mouth made her empty stomach roll.

"You are Mrs. Ross, and you shouldn't pull at the IV like that. You will injure your hand. Your nose is already bleeding from yanking out your oxygen supply. If you don't behave, Mrs. Ross, we will have to strap your hands in place so you can't injure yourself further."

"Like hell!" Lexie couldn't make her comment have the intended impact; her throat felt raw, and her voice came out scratchy, barely above a whisper. She tried again. "I am not Mrs. Anybody; my name is Alexandra Pa….” Then her voice just gave out. She watched the doctor move closer.

“Alexandra, I’m Doctor Callahan, and Nurse Thacker is correct you need to calm down. You’ve been very ill with pneumonia and will need to be with us a while longer.”

Lexie didn’t feel threatened by the tall slim slightly bald doctor with the warm brown eyes that were a close match to his sparse hair, but she didn’t trust the bossy nurse. She closed her eyes to block them out, but continued to eavesdrop on their conversation.

“Do you think she has amnesia, Doctor?”

“I doubt it, she’s most likely disoriented. Call her Alexandra when you speak to her. You can shut down the oxygen; she’s breathing fine on her own. I’ll check back before I leave tonight.”

“Maybe when her husband visits tonight it will help her memory.”

What the hell was happening? Lexie wondered as she eased into sleep.

Time has absolutely no meaning to the unconscious, or those wrapped in the blanket of a deep sleep. Lexie was coaxed from her slumber by a familiar voice accompanied by a warming sensation radiating from her right hand straight to the core of her being. Once more, her eyes scanned the room. It appeared the same, but it was hard to tell what time of day it was. She glanced down to find the source of warmth was a much larger and darker hand enfolding hers. Much as she had done earlier with the IV, she traced the appendage to its source where her gaze collided with a pair of smoky gray eyes smiling back at her. She didn’t have a clue as to the identity of the hunk with the dark brown hair and devilish grin. His too handsome face was deeply tanned with small lines that fanned out from his intriguing eyes, like he spent a lot of time squinting in the hot sun. She made a futile attempt to extricate her trapped hand, but he wasn't ready to relinquish it.

"Welcome back, Lex. How are you feeling?"

She knew the deep voice, but couldn't recall from where. There was absolutely nada familiar about the man from whom it emanated. Her voice came out a little stronger this time, but not by much. "Okay, who are you?"

"I'm crushed, Lex, that you don't remember me, after all we've been through together."

He didn't look crushed to her. His grin had broadened, accompanied by an amused twinkle in his eyes, and not a soul on earth had ever called her Lex.

"Just your name, smart ass."

"Well, I reckon 'smart ass' is better than being called a dumb ass, but my name is Cutter."

"That's it Cutter? What kind of a name is that?"

"Originally it was my mothers maiden name, but it's my given name. My last name is Ross."

Ross, Ross. Why was that familiar? "Ross! Maybe you can explain why people around here are calling me Mrs. Ross, and you can turn my hand loose."

She was definitely getting her temper up, so he opted to hold her hand a while longer in case she felt strong enough to latch on to the flower vase on the stand next to her bed and aim it at his head when he explained about her new name. "They think you're my wife because I that's what I told them the night you were admitted."

"Why would you do such a thing? I don't even know you."

"You were in no condition to talk, and admitting required insurance information."

"Your insurance carrier didn't question it?"

"I called and told them we were newlyweds and the insurance had slipped my mind during our honeymoon."

"Are you crazy? Don't you know that's fraud and you could end up in prison?"

"Doc Callahan rushed you through emergency and up to ICU. He suggested I deal with the paper maze, so I did. Claiming you as my wife was the quickest most expedient way to deal with it."

"How did we meet?"

"I plucked you out of a quagmire near a flooded creek where you were wrestling a newborn calf."

Oh my God! She realized he was the intimidating ghost rider she thought she'd conjured up in her fevered mind. "Please give me my hand back and go away. I can't deal with this now; I'm really feeling sick."

He didn't say a word, but released her hand, stood up, and left the room. Lord, when he rose from the chair she experienced an acute attack of vertigo. Sleep was a welcome escape. She couldn't remember ever being so unnerved in her twenty-four years of existence.

Cutter, however, was feeling twice his age as he forced his exhausted frame from the truck, and he'd recently turned thirty-two. A round trip to Amarillo took a four-hour bite out of his day. After the second day, when he had paced the ICU waiting area, he cut his workday short to make the trip in the evening. He'd been able to visit only ten minutes every two hours while his wife of necessity was in intensive care. He'd talked to her and stayed with her until the nurses had kicked him back to the waiting room where he would occasionally catch a catnap. Once she'd been moved into the private room, that he'd requested, he spent more time keeping vigil.

As he entered the dining room upon his return home Maria greeted him warmly. After a rib-cracking hug, she placed a bowl of stew, a piping hot mug of coffee, and a slice of apple pie on the table at his usual spot.

"Eat! You look like road kill."

He practically collapsed onto his chair. "I look that bad, huh?"

Maria sat across from him with her hands wrapped around a similar stoneware mug. "Your little mud urchin was on the news last night. Her name is Alexandra Parker, she's twenty-four and from North Olmsted, Ohio."

"She'd told me on the ride back here her name was Alexandra, but she lost consciousness before telling me more. I'd assumed by her accent when she'd been cussing out the cow, and following our subsequent brief conversation that she was a Yankee. Also, there was an Ohio plate on her Cadillac."

Maria refilled his mug and cleared his empty bowl after he declined her offer of seconds. She sat back down to fill him in while he attacked the large slice of pie. "Do you feel better now that your belly is full?"

"It sure hit the spot. Okay, spit it out, something is bothering you."

"I called the sheriff's office to report your finding the missing young woman. Patrick Boyd showed up to check it out. He contacted Dr. Joe about visiting his patient, and was told he had to wait until she regained consciousness. Since then, Alexandra's friend, the owner of the Cadillac, called the hospital only to be told that visiting was restricted to her husband. She immediately informed Patrick, who showed up here again early evening."

"What did you tell him?"

"I lied and told him I didn't know anything about it. Cutter you could be in a lot of trouble. I think what you did could be illegal."

"So I've been told."

"My Lord! Who have you told about this?"

"Alexandra."

"She is awake?"

"Oh yeah, and pissed off enough to tear a strip off my hide, if she was strong enough. Any more pie?" Cutter had a hunch that jail time was going to be the least of his problems.

CHAPTER 5

DAVID Decker fought for control over the blinding haze of rage threatening to overwhelm him. He had thought his problems were behind him when he moved in with his maternal grandmother to play caretaker and run the ranch. He'd expected a large cash inheritance in addition to the five remaining sections of the ranch when the old matriarch died, but she left a large chunk of money in trust for her other four grandchildren. Some of her accumulated wealth went to charity, but not a dime to her two sons, or her late daughter's drifter husband. Her children hadn't been able get away from the ranch fast enough. He knew he should feel grateful that there were adequate funds left to him to run what remained of the ranch. Dear old Granny Sophie sold off more than half of the place after Grandpa Karl died, a decade before her grandson had arrived on the scene. Granny was always watchful, and he'd made an effort to impress her. She had held the opinion he was too much like his father had been. A good-looking, smooth-talking conman, and she'd never forgiven her daughter for running off with his dad.

He poured another slug of the Kentucky bourbon that he favored and tried to calm down. It wouldn't be productive to lose control now. He was very close to his goal. Rich little Melinda Potter was his latest conquest. He'd spent the better part of a year courting her over the Internet and subsequent phone conversations where he spent considerable time and effort urging her to come for a visit when she graduated. He'd zeroed in on the attractive brunette after his extensive research revealed she was the only daughter of filthy rich parents. Pain radiated from his cramping belly to register in his slightly pickled mind. David cussed his fate as he scrounged through the pantry and fridge. "It's probably not the lack of food making my gut hurt, but the idea of having to marry again." His complaints went unheard in the empty house.

Gambling debts sucked up most of the cash Sophie had bequeathed him, but that didn't stop him from racking up more IOU's. He reasoned that he could sell off some the cattle at auction, but the damned drought had ranchers dumping animals left and right, so his sales were a fraction of what he'd hoped. Then, the cloudburst drowned a dozen head while he was cheering on the deluge. He'd picked up Melinda at the hotel in Lubbock for an intimate dinner and the seduction he'd planned. She'd called to cancel dinner since her friend hadn't returned with her car from a clinic visit. He figured it worked to his benefit to have Melissa dependent on him for transportation. It would allow him more time to work his wiles, but she had insisted on having Lexie join them. The roommate had taken an immediate dislike to him despite his renowned charm. He'd routed her the long way around hoping she would return to Lubbock rather than battle the building storm. She would have put a major a kink into his plans for the evening.

David felt giddy, like dancing a jig. The blonde menace was missing and had presumably gone the way of his ill-fated cattle. He almost blew it with Melinda by pushing the issue of the insurance filing. It took some quick talking to smooth that mistake over, and he decided to back off the subject for a few days. He would be there to comfort his little gold-plated heiress when Melinda's friend's body was found.

******

Lexie was feeling much better by noon of the day following her visit from Cutter. She didn't believe his explanation for the Mrs. Ross debacle, but figured she owed him for saving her twice. Later that afternoon when Melinda showed up with a deputy sheriff in tow, Lexie played the dumb blonde stereotype to the hilt.

Melinda stood in the room gawking at her, and then the dam burst. "Lexie, you scared the hell out of me! I thought you were dead. You look like crap! Oh, by the way, this is Deputy Sheriff Patrick Boyd. You should see the photos of the Escalade, and then you would realize how terrified I was. I'm so sorry I badgered you into making that awful trip. Why are you listed as Mrs. Ross? Just who is Mr. Ross?"

The deputy was intent on the little blonde's reaction to Melinda's rapid-fire string of questions. Lexie nodded to him in recognition of their brief introduction. Suddenly, it was quiet. Her hyper friend had fallen silent and was waiting for Lexie's response.

She tried to remember the list her friend had presented like a radio commercial disclaimer. "I'm sorry you were frightened, and thanks for your assessment of my appearance." Lexie was gratified to see Melinda look a bit chagrined. "Actually, I'm told I look much better today. I am sorry about losing your SUV. Nice to meet you, Deputy Boyd, I think."

Patrick found it interesting that Lexie didn't answer Melinda's question about her marital status, so he broached the omission. "Alexandra, should I put your last name on my report as Parker or Ross?"

"Take your pick, Deputy Boyd, everyone else does."

He took note of her cryptic remark and pursued it. "When did you marry Cutter Ross?"

"You know, I really don't remember. I only came around yesterday, and everyone was calling me Mrs. Ross. I think the high fever scrambled my gray matter. Things are out of sequence; it's hard for me to decide what was real and what was a fever-induced hallucination. I guess you'll have to ask Cutter."

"I'll wait for you in the lobby, Melinda. Pleasure to meet you, Lexie."

He fully intended to have a talk with Cutter; the whole story just didn't add up. Patrick had a feeling she could remember more than she was willing to admit.

Once he was out of the room, Lexie seized the offensive. "Who's the uniform, Melinda? Have you been spending a lot of time with him?"

"Lexie! He's the law. Deputy Boyd has been keeping me informed on the search for you. I think he was expecting to recover a body until yesterday. How are you really?"

"I'm better. They've removed most of the damned tubes, and I can go to the bathroom now. I just have to roll the IV tree along with me. I had some broth and Jell-O today. Mel, do me a favor, bring me something to wear that won't cause your lawman friend to arrest me for mooning folks."

"Stop stalling, Lexie, tell me about Ross."

"Can't. I don't know anything about him. I'm really beat, Mel, and could use some sleep before I have to deal with my new husband this evening."

Melinda left Lexie and retreated, temporarily, to join the deputy. Like him, she had a feeling Lexie was hiding something. Mel chalked the short visit up to the questions she'd been asking about her recently resurrected friend's mysterious husband.

A more agreeable nurse—Thacker was either not on duty or had the day off—gave her some ibuprofen for the throbbing between her ears. The verbal sparring with Melinda and the deputy had depleted her limited supply of energy. Lexie dozed off following a bland liquid dinner. She didn't resurface from her deep dreamless sleep until the following morning. Once she verified that it was indeed morning, she wondered if Cutter had shown up the previous evening.

******

He'd been working for hours by the time Lexie was served breakfast. Cutter straddled the bales on the truck bed as the vehicle bounced along between hay feeders, strategically placed near dwindling water supplies, while Jim drove. Usually, he rode in the cab with Jim, but Cutter wasn't fit company for man or beast.

Jim exited the cab at each stop to cut the bailing strings and pull them from the feeder while his taciturn boss tossed in the bales. Jim knew something was eating at the other man. Cutter wasn't the gabby type, but he was exceptionally quiet that morning. He either barked orders as if he was a drill instructor, or growled like a bear when he did speak.

Cutter worked like a man possessed—an attempt to relieve the stress that had been building since the previous evening when Patrick Boyd waylaid him. Cutter had been fresh from the shower and looking forward to a quick dinner before making the trip to Amarillo. He'd run into a roadblock in the form of the deputy who was seated at the kitchen table. Maria had invited Patrick to dinner. Cutter squelched the nagging feeling that the invite had been more of an attempt to keep him from making the trip to the hospital than it was a simple act of hospitality.

The two men had waltzed around the subject of Cutter's new wife through the course of the meal. He'd been shown the photos of the recovered Escalade. The mere thought that she could have been in that mangled wreck, had Momma cow not been blocking the road, turned the tender cut of beef and Spanish rice into hot lead in his belly. Boyd had been quick to pick up on his reaction.

"Maria gave me a brief account of what happened when Alexandra arrived here. How did you meet her, Cutter?"

Ross went over the story that had been replaying since he viewed the graphic photos.

"Did the two of you have a previous history?"

Lexie was right; his ass was going to jail. "What did she tell you?"

"Alexandra claimed she couldn't recall. She gave me some excuse about a high fever scrambling her brains, and then she suggested I ask you when I questioned her about whether her last name was Parker or Ross. Which is it Cutter?"

"Why don't you put Parker hyphen Ross in your report and let it go at that."

Boyd was like a dog with a bone; he kept gnawing away. "When exactly did the two of you tie the knot?"

"Recently."

"Newlyweds, huh?"

"Right."

Cutter had reverted to one-word answers. He'd been straining to look casual and unaffected by the line of questioning. He'd also made note of the grin on the deputy's face as he dug into the slice of strawberry pie. Cutter hadn't admitted anything to their dinner guest, but his gut told him that Boyd knew precisely what was going on and found the situation humorous. Warmth flowed over him as he thought about Lexie playing dumb to protect what she'd referred to as his dumb ass.

It had been too late to make the trip to check on her by the time Patrick departed. He'd consoled himself with the idea that someone from the hospital would call him should she make a turn for the worse. He'd worked off his frustration by loading the trucks with hay for the morning run to replenish the feeders scattered around the ranch. What little fresh grass produced by the inland bands of the last tropical storm was now history. The flash floods barely dented the persistent drought and continued to make the purchase of hay an expensive necessity. Hay from out of state was sure putting a strain on the ranch's operational budget, but he was going to have to order more or let the stock starve.

Cutter called a halt after lunch, cleaned up and refreshed he headed north. Lexie wasn't in her room when he arrived. Nurse Thacker directed him down the hall to a solarium where he found her in the company of a brunette with a couple of more vertical inches than Lexie, who was about his shoulder height. She spotted him before he entered the sunlit room and blushed a color similar to the frilly rose robe she wore over a lacey pink nightgown. He made an attempt not to grin, but failed miserably.

"Afternoon, ladies. Lex, you aren't overdoing it are you?"

She probably was, but she wouldn't admit it to him. The short walk down here from her claustrophobic cell had her puffing like she had just run a marathon. Carting the rolling IV tree along didn't help the situation either. She'd collapsed into one of soft upholstered chairs as soon as she and Mel had reached the small haven. It felt wonderful to bask in the sun streaming through the huge tinted windows. She must be feeling stronger, she thought—either that or her mind had snapped. If he didn't stop grinning at her and ogling her horrid pink outfit, she was going to get out of this comfy chair and smack him right upside his head. She graced him with her most defiant glare.

"I am just fine. Thank you for your concern." He was now eying her skeptically. She thought an introduction was in order. Once Mel found out who he was, Cutter would be too busy fielding questions to keep perusing her with his intriguing and unsettling gray eyes. "Mel, this is Cutter Ross. Cutter, meet my friend and roommate Melinda Potter."

Cutter nodded a brief recognition following the introduction, then turned his attention back to assessing her. Mel came through and then some. Cutter was unprepared for Lexie's friend to hop out of her chair throwing her arms around his neck then kissing him smack on the mouth.

"Welcome to the family, Cutter! I really should be bummed at you for not inviting me to the wedding, but you're too cute to stay angry at."

Lexie was the one grinning now. He looked confused, a bit shell shocked, or like he'd just been hit by an angry bull. Lexie didn't think anyone had called Cutter 'cute' since he was a small child, if then. Mel also noticed his confusion.

"You are the right Mr. Ross, aren't you? The one who's supposed to be Lexie's husband?"

"Right."

"Exactly when was the wedding?"

"Recently."

Melinda looked to her friend for direction. Her husband, if he was, refused to embellish on his one-word responses. It was down right frustrating. "Lexie, is he always this talkative?"

Lexie shrugged her shoulders and looked him in the eye. "Beats me, Mel, I can't remember a thing."

Mel stomped her foot with hands on her hips, and glared accusingly at Lexie. "Don't give me that crap! You never forget anything, but you don't remember getting hitched? Do you expect me to buy that?"

"You bought Decker's line of crap enough to travel across the country. So why can't you believe I don't remember everything that happened after I buried your ride in the muck, and then woke up in the hospital? Have I ever lied to you?"

Cutter was not happy with the turn of events. The blush had disappeared from Lexie's cheeks to be replaced with a pasty pallor reminiscent of the days she had a machine breathing for her. So he sat in the chair next to her, picked up her right hand, and that was when David Decker entered. It was as if the women had conjured him up. Cutter observed as Melinda exuberantly launched herself at the new arrival, much as she'd done to him a few minutes earlier. Decker returned the embrace and kissed her, but Cutter noticed the lack of warmth in the other man's eyes. He recognized a cold and calculating look that belonged in a boardroom negotiating deals, not in the embrace of a beautiful woman. Holding Lexie's hand, he was aware of the instant tension in her when Decker entered the room.

David's appearance effectively dampened her spirits and turned her stomach. Lexie felt as if she'd let the Potter's down. In her mind, she owed Mel's parents a huge debt since they had assisted with her pursuit of a business degree. Mr. Potter had arranged an unprecedented paying internship for her with one of his businesses in Columbus. The internship with a prestigious CPA firm gave her practical experience and much better pay than her previous job as a waitress. That debt of gratitude was the reason she had agreed to the Texas trip. Mel was impulsive when it came to a lot of things in life, including her relationships with men. Melinda's prime focus at OSU had been to find Mr. Right before she graduated while Lexie was busy working her way through college,

"Cutter, would you walk back to my room with me? I think I've had all I can stand for today."

He stayed to her right side while she manipulated the IV stand with her left hand. She was a little wobbly as she gained her feet and latched onto his left arm to steady herself. He had a little difficulty adjusting his stride to her smaller halting steps. All in all, he thought she did okay for her first walk about. The brief farewell between the friends was strained, but more interesting was that not a word had passed between Lex and Decker. The animosity directed at her from the other man was palpable. He had a hunch Decker would have been a lot happier had Lex remained in the Escalade to its end. Her return from the small restroom put an end to his speculation.

She really disliked the nurse on duty and was attempting to coerce him into helping her out of the rose-colored robe. Cutter was uneasy about assisting her with removing her robe, which entailed clamping the IV to get her left arm out. Fortunately, Nurse Thacker arrived to finish the honors. He was so happy to see the nurse enter the room that he could have kissed her. Lex'd insisted the two of them could manage and there wasn't a reason to bother the nurse.

Thacker's squeaky little girl voice irritated Lexie, especially when the matronly nurse tried bossing her around. She found it difficult to control her ire when the hefty woman threatened her with dire circumstances—like strapping her wrists to the bed—if she didn't toe the mark. Lexie had to put up with that kind of scolding from her grandmother, but she didn't intend to take it from this pain in the posterior. Once she was safely in bed, the nurse hung the robe in a small closet, and placed the fuzzy rose slippers on the floor beneath it. Thacker turned to assess Lexie.

"You know, Mrs. Ross, pink is not your color. It does absolutely nothing for you."

"I agree. You should give your fashion tips to my friend the next time she comes."

The nurse ignored Lexie's sarcastic response, and turned her attention to Cutter. "Mr. Ross, the dinner trays will be arriving shortly; would you like me to put in an order for you? You can share dinner with you wife."

Cutter glanced over at Lexie for some guidance and found her shaking her head while mouthing 'no'. So, of course he accepted the nurse's offer. Lexie didn't even wait for the nurse to exit before calling him to task.

"Are you nuts? That stuff will probably give you food poisoning. Then you'll end up in here too."

"Do you think they'll let us share?"

"Not going to happen. This is a private room, or don't you remember, Mr. Big Spender?"

"I remember. I thought your condition warranted a relatively quiet private room."

"It's going to take me years to pay this back. Melinda is the rich one, not me."

"Your friend is rich?" No wonder Sophie's narcissistic grandson is so interested, he thought.

"Well, her parents are. The Cadillac I trashed was her graduation gift from them. Are you wishing you would have responded a bit more enthusiastically when she wrapped her arms around you?"

"Melinda isn't my type. Besides, I'm a married man."

"Oh really! What is your type, Mr. Ross?"

"You, Lex."

They were interrupted by the arrival of the dinner trays. Lexie was treated to beef broth, lime Jell-O, some strange-looking pureed meat that was supposed to be pot roast, mashed potatoes with an eye dropper full of gravy, and a yellow-orange vegetable that the menu declared to be carrots. Her taste buds didn't register any of the semi-soft offerings; every bite was bland. Cutter's pot roast was at least recognizable, as were his carrots. He enjoyed a hefty helping of gravy on his mashed potatoes, and a slice of devil's food cake that made her mouth water. At least the warm cup of tea hit the spot. Strong willpower and the need to extricate her frail self from this torture chamber compelled her to clean up the slop on her tray.

Cutter disappeared after the trays were picked up. Lexie maneuvered until her bare toes touched the ground, and then made her way to the bathroom. The simplest tasks seemed to wear her out. She thought he'd gone for the night, or she would have grabbed the damn rose robe. Cutter was again seated in the chair beside her bed by the time she exited the necessary room. Melinda's lacy pink nightgown didn't hide much. As quickly as she could manage she positioned the IV stand next to the bed and scooted under the covers. Cutter returned with a cup of tea, a Dixie cup of chocolate ice cream for her, a large coffee for himself, and a deck of cards.

"Where did you get this stuff?"

"The cafeteria on the first level, except the deck of cards. Got them at the gift shop. Do you play?" He raised one of his dark eyebrows and grinned when he asked the question.

"Play what exactly?"

"Cards, of course. What's your game?"

She had the feeling there was a double entendre behind that question. "Solitaire."

Cutter gave her a skeptical look, but bit back the first retort that came to mind knowing she would take exception to it. "That's it? Just solitaire?"

"I can play a little rummy, passable poker, and canasta."

Rummy was the choice. On his way out, he told her the cards were hers and that perhaps she could drum up a game with some other patsy. It was a good thing she refused to play for money, or she'd now own the ranch.

He mulled over their conversation during his fleecing by the pint sized card shark. She had been on the way to Decker's, at Melinda's request, when she'd come to the lower crossroads. She'd backed out when it became apparent the road had washed away. Once out, she headed for high ground where she'd ended up in a confrontation with one of his cows. Lex was sure that Decker had deliberately given her incorrect directions. Cutter tended to agree with her assessment. She'd been traveling from Lubbock to the Lazy K ranch house. The question nagging at Cutter was, why she'd ended up so far out in the wrong direction?

CHAPTER 6

L EXIE woke to the sound of breakfast trays being pulled from large stainless steel warmers. She wolfed down her breakfast of oatmeal, applesauce, and orange juice. She then gathered her toiletries and took the long slow walk down the hall to the showers.

The slightly hot spray warmed deep through to her soul. A tingling sensation spread out from her vigorously messaged scalp. Once She'd been relieved of the IV, a shower had moved to the top of her wish list. Sponge baths had been a trial, and she was grateful she could only remember the past few days. She estimated she'd been confined to the hospital for at least a week, but only the last three days were clear. Before that everything was bits of clarity, foggy impressions, and disembodied voices.

Her skin began to feel too tight and the room seemed to be shrinking. She went from pacing the confines her room to pacing the hall. She spent more time in the solarium reading or playing solitaire. She hadn't had a visitor in the past two days. Melinda wasn't responding to her cell phone or the landline at the hotel. Lexie didn't know the number at the ranch or Cutter's cell number, and she was not about to ask anyone at the hospital. They already thought she had brain damage thanks to Cutter claiming her as his wife.

Lexie took her deck of cards with her down to the solarium. If she couldn't find anything interesting to read, she would occupy herself with a few games of solitaire. Tinted glass kept out the harsh glare of the sun, and she enjoyed spending a little time here each day. It was a pleasant relief from her antiseptic white on white room. Vinyl, upholstered, armchairs in multiple colors of pastels were scattered around three sides of the room in cozy pairs. Small Formica tables were strategically placed with magazines and newspapers holding them in place. Silk ferns hung from brass pots positioned over the small tables. A couple of larger tables took up part of the floor space in the center of the pleasant room where patients often worked on puzzles, or like her played cards. She decided on a National Geographic that she had not yet read and settled into her usual chair.

I probably am scrambled beneath my squeaky clean scalp, Lexie thought. She actually experienced joy at the arrival of Deputy Boyd. He sat in the chair Cutter had occupied on her first trip to this glassed in view of the outside world. The apparent purpose of the deputy's visit was to return her recovered handbag.

"Why didn't you return it the last time you were here?"

"Your bag and the contents were waterlogged and coated with mud from being submerged for a prolonged period. I kept it until things were dried out and cleaned up some. It was fortunate your ID was in it; had we not recovered that you would still be a missing person. Worst case, you could have been presumed dead."

Lexie could imagine the heartache her mother and grandmother would have experienced. "Well, I thank you for not giving up, Deputy." She changed the subject hoping he could shed some light on Mel's whereabouts. "Deputy, have you seen or heard from Melinda in the past two days?"

"No. Why?"

"She left here with David Decker three days ago, and I haven't been able to contact her since. I'm really worried about her. It isn't like her to be out of touch."

"I'll swing by the hotel to check it out."

"Thank you."

Lexie took an inventory of her returned items. Most of the photos, her note pad, business cards, and hospital insurance card were ruined. But her laminated driver's license, student ID, and plastic credit card had survived intact. In the future, anything of importance was getting laminated.

After lunch, once the nurse and lab techs were done poking her, she pulled on the rose robe and stepped into the slippers to go on a walkabout. She wasn't paid much attention. The staff had become used to her pacing the halls. She found an ATM five floors down and added to the forty dollars in the rock hard leather wallet she'd stuffed in a large pocket of the robe. Lexie figured her next step was to locate the gift shop. She needed the blissful oblivion of a long afternoon nap by the time she stashed her purchases upon returning to her room,

She woke to the sound of male voices and pretended sleep in order to eavesdrop on their conversation. She tried not to groan out loud when Dr. Callahan said he wanted to keep her four or five more days to run some additional tests. The disturbing discussion ended and the sound of footsteps exited her immediate vicinity, their echo fading down the hall. A frown creased her brow as she considered her options.

"Are you frowning because you're in pain, Lex, or because you didn't like Callahan's plans for more tests?"

Her eyes popped open at the sound of his voice, and she stared into laughing gray eyes. He was towering over the foot of bed.

"Both. Please sit down, I'm getting dizzy having to crane my neck to look up at you."

He complied with her wish and sat in the chair to her right as usual. Once they were on a bit more of an equal level, she broached the subject of communications. "I thought you had forgotten me. Give me your cell number before you head home tonight in case I have to get in touch with you."

"Sorry, I'm a little shorthanded right now, and got bogged down. Why didn't you ask the doctor or Nurse Thacker for my number, they both have it?"

"Do you even have to ask? Callahan will be ordering brain scans if your wife can't recall your cell or the ranch phone numbers." She wanted to smack the grin off his face, but restrained the urge. She wasn't in a position to make a hasty escape, and at that moment he was jotting down the requested numbers. Cutter had no more than handed the ranch business card to her complete with his cell number scrawled on the back when Deputy Boyd strolled in.

"Evening, folks. Hope I'm not interrupting."

Lexie stashed the business card under her pillow while the deputy pulled a chair to the opposite side of her bed from where Cutter sat. She was sure the deputy would find it odd that a husband would hand his wife his business card. Once seated, Boyd pulled out his little notepad. Lexie figured in the age of iPhones and Droids he used the old fashioned form of note taking as an intimidation factor.

"I checked into the whereabouts of your friend."

"Did you find her?"

"According to the doorman at the hotel where the two of you had been staying until your recent nuptials." Patrick couldn't resist the little dig at Cutter. "Melinda entered with a man of Decker's description within hours of departing from her visit with you and hasn't been back since. She left with a small overnight bag and a cosmetic case. I went out to Decker's place. He wasn't there either. An old ranch hand said he went to San Antonio with his new lady friend. He didn't know the lady's name, but what he recalled of her physical appearance fits Melinda."

"Okay, but why can't I reach her? She's never without her phone."

"There have been a number of communication problems around this part of Texas. Some cell towers were damaged by recent wildfires, and others were pulled down by flashflood debris. Most are back up, but there are still service outages in some areas. It's possible the spotty service could be the reason for your inability to reach her."

"Did you search our room? She might have left it behind—on the charger or something."

"Sorry Mrs. Ross. I couldn't search the room without an official investigation and a warrant." Patrick couldn't resist placing an emphasis on the Mrs. Ross when he addressed Lexie. Though he never took his eyes from her, his peripheral vision took note of Cutter's reactions.

"There must be something we can do. I really don't trust David."

"Unfortunately, our gut feelings aren't enough to initiate a full investigation. Keep me advised if you hear from her, and I'll do likewise."

Cutter waited until the deputy departed the room to question her. Over twin dinner trays, she caught him up on the happenings of the past two and a half days since she'd last seen him. She plotted her course for the next day once Cutter left for home. Lexie prayed she had enough strength and money to manage the long cab ride back to Lubbock.

******

Lexie went on her usual post-breakfast walk with her storm battered handbag stuffed beneath her robe. Once the coast was clear, she eased into the next available elevator on its way down.

An elderly couple already in the conveyance didn't pay the least bit of attention to her bulging rose robe.

Lexie exited one floor up from the lobby to stuff the robe in a trash receptacle. Only one more floor then out through the busy lobby, she thought. Lexie hoped she wouldn't be too conspicuous when she exited the elevator. Her light blue gift shop tee declared, in bold read letters, "Don't mess with Texas." Her T-shirt sort of coordinated with a baggy pair of red boxer shorts she had purchased. However, the red clashed big time with the fuzzy rose slippers she was forced to wear or go barefoot. She held her breath as she exited the front entrance, but not a single person paid the least bit of attention to her. Luck was with her and the cab she had called from her room arrived as she exited the prison like structure. She noticed the cabbie gave her a look, like she was an escapee from a loony bin. The thought occurred to Lexie that his perception wasn't really too far from the truth. It wasn't her strange footwear that concerned the cab driver, but her stated destination.

At least thirty miles passed in the air-conditioned cab on her long ride to the hotel before she felt the tension melt from her body. Once able to relax, she dozed off for the remainder of the trip. She emerged from her slumber when the cab halted. It took most of her funds to pay for the ride and leave a skimpy tip. The doorman was the first to notice her strange attire; he was used to seeing her dressed like she just stepped out of a fashion magazine. She was grateful he didn't ask any questions, such as where she had been for so long. A thought flitted through her mind: Mel had probably filled him and everyone else in on recent events. Worn out, she was looking forward to a relaxing shower, some lunch, and a nap before attempting to locate a new iPhone. Mel's voice reached her ears as she stepped through the door of their shared accommodations. Lexie placed her shoulder bag on the desk next to her friend's laptop, and then proceeded to open the door to their bedroom. Her expectation had been to find Mel perhaps conversing with someone on her phone. The sight of her nude friend in bed having sex with David Decker hit her with the impact of a knock out punch!

******

Cutter and Sam were assessing yearling and two-year old horses they'd penned up. His cell startled him as well as a young stud colt they were evaluating. Aggravated, he growled into the offending device, "WHAT?"

Twenty minutes later, he was setting land speed records for the trip to Amarillo. It was his custom to adjust the phone to vibrate, especially when working with green horses, but occasionally he would miss a call, which was not usually a major deal. He could always call back at a more opportune time. Considering Lexie's condition since she slid into his life, he'd kept the volume turned up. He didn't have the time or patience to mess with one of the phones with all the apps and functions. A basic push key cell with minimal functions served his purposes: emergency use and the ability to remain accessible.

Once he finally reached the hospital, he checked her room, the halls, and the solarium. Cutter extended the search to the cafeteria as well as the gift shop. It was at the shop that he picked up a clue to her disappearance. The clerk remembered a young lady who matched Lexie's description had made a purchase of some clothing items yesterday afternoon. She'd paid cash for the items. Maybe she'd taken my joke to heart and fleeced some unsuspecting card players, he speculated. Wherever she got the funds it was obvious, to him, she'd planned her getaway. He was on his way to the information desk in the lobby when his cell went off again. "What?"

"WOW! Do you always answer your phone like that?"

He took his first relaxed breath in hours, and the ache between his shoulder blades began to ease. "Lex! Where in the hell are you?"

"In Lubbock. I wanted to call you before you headed to the hospital, if that was on your agenda this evening."

"Too late, but I appreciate the thought. Give me the address and stay put until I get there."

******

Lexie gave him the address of the hotel. She'd agreed to meet him in the

Restaurant off the lobby, and then ordered lunch. She figured nurse Thacker had probably called him when Lexie wasn't there for the tests doc had scheduled. Her pretend husband hadn't sounded happy and his voice turned to a low-pitched growl when she'd informed him that if he showed up with the ambulance—as suggested by Doc Callahan —she wouldn't be here. He'd sworn, to her, no ambulance would show up. Then he repeated his command to stay put. Lexie wished she had the strength and wherewithal to leave Texas. However, she was in short supply of energy as well as funds. She had run out of options and couldn't, in good conscience, leave Lubbock until she exhausted all possibilities to extricate Mel from David's clutches.

She picked at her salad while she recalled the earlier confrontation with Mel and David. Her relief at discovering her friend had returned was short-lived. The fact that she found Mel in a compromising situation with her cyber-Romeo had fired Lexie's notoriously bad temper. She gave them five minutes to get up and get dressed. Mel came out in a pink robe reminiscent of the rose one occupying a trash can at the hospital, and she too was on the warpath. Lexie demanded to know why Decker was in their shared bedroom. They'd agreed no men in the suite, let alone the bedroom. To that Mel replied, "My parents are footing the bill for this place, and I can have anyone I wish stay over. If you don't like how I chose to spend my time you can move out."

She gathered her belongings and packed her clothes while David looked on with a smug expression, still sprawled under the sheets. Lixie wished she were in decent shape, and not on the verge of collapse. She would've really enjoyed putting a world of hurt on the creep. A hotel valet had responded to her call and loaded her luggage onto a cart, and then escorted her down to the lobby. There she'd officially checked out and made the call to Cutter.

He arrived much sooner than she had anticipated, and she was having second thoughts about her decision to call him. His countenance could have been chiseled out of stone, except for a fascinating tick in his jaw. It didn't escape her notice that his normally warm smoky eyes appeared glacial. Lexie fought the urge to shiver. "Have you had lunch, Cutter?"

"No. I was hightailing it to Amarillo well before our usual lunch break."

"I'm sorry, but it's your own fault. If you hadn't told them I was your wife, they wouldn't have called you just because I took an extended walk. I did try to head you off."

"You call this an extended walk?" He was growling at her.

"It wasn't necessary for you to come here." Her tone became belligerent; she stiffened her spine, and glared right back into his stormy face.

"Can it, Lex. Why are you hanging out down here instead of resting in your room?"

"I checked out."

"Why?"

"If you order something to eat, it may improve your disposition. I'll update you on events while you have lunch."

He worked on the biggest burger she'd ever seen while she brought him up to speed. She explained that since Deputy Boyd couldn't search their room she felt that she had to do it. Her friend had returned, but not alone. Lexie guided him through the nasty confrontation and up to the present.

"Suppose I hadn't shown up, what was your plan?"

"First, I was going to rent a car, and then try to replace my phone that is either still buried deep in the muck on your ranch or went the way of Mel's Cadillac. Also, I planned to find a more affordable place to live while I hunt for a for a bookkeeping or entry level accounting job."

"That's pretty ambitious for someone barely off life support."

"Maybe I'm not a hundred percent, but hanging around that hospital wasn't doing me any good, and it isn't like I am looking for a physically demanding job. Another day or two of that hospital routine and I would have had to be fitted for a straight jacket."

"As it happens, I know of someone in desperate need of an accountant, or at the very least a competent bookkeeper, to sort out their business dealings. Can you handle it?"

"I've had some experience in that area. How bad is it?"

"I'll set up an interview for tomorrow. You'll want to get a good night of rest and be fresh. Let's see about replacing your phone for starters."

"What about the rental car?"

"If you get the job, there will be plenty of time to worry about renting a car. In the mean time you can use mine."

Though reluctant to be in his debt further she realized her options, as well as her strength were severely limited at the moment. She nodded her aching head, "Fine"

Lexie was able to acquire a new iPhone at a reduced price since she'd had the good sense to purchase insurance on the previous one. At the time, she'd been more concerned with its theft than the hazard of mud and floods halfway across the U.S. What she wasn't prepared for was returning to Cutter's ranch for the night. He was right; she was too tired to look for lodgings, and he refused to even consider letting her find another hotel or motel for the night. He offered to loan her the Yukon they were traveling in, and he insisted that the interview would be much closer to his ranch. She didn't remember much about her arrival or the short time she had spent there. She did recall the middle of nowhere feeling she'd experienced while trying to find Decker's place. The same sensation once again assailed her, but the dust following in the wake of his silver Yukon was the polar opposite of the monsoon she'd tried to navigate through that day. Parched, cracked, and heaved up in spots the ground seemed to scream, "ankle breaker!" The landscape as far as she could see begged for rain. "What do the livestock eat? I don't see a blade of grass anywhere."

"There isn't much left—drought and wildfires have devastated a large area of the state. Agriculture is in the toilet. Farmers and ranchers are struggling just to survive. Most can't afford to bring in hay from outside of Texas, so they're dumping their stock at sales. It's that or watch them starve."

Their conversation ceased as the ranch outbuildings began to materialize out of the parched landscape. Lexie knew she'd been here before, but seeing it in the glare of the hot afternoon sun took some getting used to. Waves of heat undulated from the scorched earth distorting the lines of the house and barns. She squinted her eyes in an effort to get a better view. She was still rubbernecking when she realized Cutter was unloading her luggage. Like a sleepwalker rudely awakened, she grabbed her overnight case, mangled shoulder bag, and her invaluable laptop. She followed him up the stone walkway to the covered porch of the white stucco house with its terracotta-colored roof tiles.

Then she proceeded through the front door as he held it open. Nothing looked the least bit familiar, but then from what she'd been able to piece together from Cutter's sparse accounts, they had entered from the far side of the house through the mudroom on her first visit to his home.

More aware this time, she took in the sprawling footprint of the house. She thought it curious that there wasn't a tree, a flowerbed, or even a rock garden with cacti that she's noticed around the homes and businesses in Lubbock. She'd seen similar landscaping around the hospital when she made her escape. She followed him down a wide hall, for now she could only guess at the rooms to the left of the central hall; the right side seemed to be mostly sleeping quarters. Cutter opened a door near the back of the house. He stashed her luggage on the closet floor.

"It stays cooler at the back of the house away from the kitchen, Lex. You have time to take a shower, rest for a while, or unpack a few things before dinner. I'll see you later."

The room was decorated in cool blues and greens. There were no curtains, only vertical blinds in a light green that coordinated with the blue and green spread. Pillow shams that matched decorated the double bed. Walls were painted a pale blue that was nearly white. Several braided throw rugs with the same color scheme were scattered on the white and gray terrazzo floor. The floor down the long hall had been the same kind of surface, but was more of a tan color. The predominately white floor flowed into the attached bath. A shower had been on the top of her list once she got back to the hotel, but things went south from there. She placed her terrycloth robe on the back of the door. There was a duplicate brass hook on the other door. Curious, she opened it to peek in. Okay, it looked like the bath was shared, so she closed the door over before locking it, and then made quick work of her shower. Terry robe in place, she unlocked the door to the adjoining room before retreating to her temporary bedchamber to blow-dry her hair. Clean and braided her hair was beginning to feel normal once more. A navy tank and a pair of denim cutoffs replaced her damp robe. Shoeless, Lexie stretched across the inviting bed; she was out as soon as she closed her eyes.

She'd become accustomed to waking to Cutter's image beside her bed and it took a few moments for her to realize she was no longer in the hospital. The instant she remembered where she was, she also became aware he was sitting on the foot of the bed she was sprawled across.

"Are you ready to join the rest of us for dinner, Sleeping Beauty?"

Maria's cooking was a world away from the bland hospital fare. The meal caused her to rethink Cutter's motivation to share hospital dinner trays with her. She wolfed down the spicy burritos, Spanish rice, and garden salad loaded with a con queso style dressing that was offered for the evening's dinner as if she were a starving person. Lexie was sure she was going to pay for her overindulgence with a bellyache, but the spicy food was such a treat. However, one swig of the iced tea almost brought everything she had eaten to the recycle receptacle located in the attached bath at the other end of the house. Fortunately, her still touchy stomach settled and she was spared the humiliation of making an emergency dash down the hall. She switched to water.

CHAPTER 7

L EXIE made quick work of breakfast early the next morning, around seven. Bacon and scrambled eggs evaporated as if by magic, and she was working on her second cup of hair curling coffee. She ate alone; it appeared Cutter and Maria's husband were out checking on stock before even respectable roosters were up and crowing. Maria sat and had a cup of coffee with her. She had a distinct feeling that the older woman was evaluating more than her ratty old jeans and oversized blue T-shirt, or physical condition. It was over coffee that Lexie discovered the dark honey skinned cook with the plump Dolly Parton profile and eyes nearly as dark as her raven colored hair was to be her escort to the interview at ten thirty. Lexie wondered if Maria would also be making introductions to her prospective employer. She had espected Cutter to accompany her to the interview.

At 8:30 AM Texas time, Lexie called her mom at work to let her know she was out of the hospital. It had taken all her strength when she woke there to sound normal when she called home. It took some fast-talking to convince Mom and Grandma she was fine and there wasn't any reason to make the trip to Texas. She told her mom she was feeling much better and even had a job interview scheduled for that morning. Then Lexie made the obligatory call to Melinda's parents. Fortunately, Ohio operated on Eastern Time, making it an hour later and the Potter's were at the law office. A half-hour later, after explaining about her ill-fated trip to join their daughter for dinner and her prolonged stay at the hospital, she took them through the confrontation with Mel the day before. Lexie suggested they intervene. "I'm worried about her, Mr. Potter. She didn't look right to me, like she was on something. He has undue influence over her."

"Do you think he drugged her?"

Lexie tried to remember the physical appearance of her friend during their confrontation. "I can't prove anything, but Mel's strange behavior would make more sense. Her eyes did appear way too dilated for the light in the sitting room where we had our disagreement. I don't trust him and wouldn't put anything past him."

Benson felt responsible for Lexie's brush with death. Spoiled and willful his only daughter was used to having her own way. It had probably not been fair for his wife, Linda, and him to have saddle Lexie with trying to keep Melinda out of trouble. "How are you, Lexie?"

"I think escaping from the hospital yesterday was, in hindsight, good in some aspects. I'm staying temporarily with a local family that I got to know while at the hospital, and I have a job interview in less than an hour, near here. Wish me luck."

"Good luck, Lexie. Let us know if you need references. We'll be in touch soon."

Guilt was her companion as she dressed for her interview, but she took some comfort in the realization that she would feel a lot worse if something terrible were to happen to Mel. David's power over her friend had gone beyond any sway Lexie may have had in quelling the relationship.

She'd managed a decent rendition of a french braid, but found the chore extremely taxing. She darkened her eyebrows and applied a light pink lip stain. She opted out of makeup even though she was pathetically pale; the heat would only sweat it from her face. What little tan she had going when she first arrived in this godforsaken land had been lost between the sheets of an Amarillo hospital bed. The figure in the mirror over the small white dressing table looked presentable, if not as professional as she would have liked. A white cotton tank top supplied minimal contrast to her makeup-less complexion. Her white top set off the hunter green slacks. She chose an antique gold locket and slipped her grandmother's gold watch on her left wrist, grateful that she'd left them behind on the day of her mud bath. Her only other jewelry consisted of the small gold studs in her ears. She fingered them and wondered where her small diamond earrings had ended up. It was the first she'd remembered that she had worn them for her fateful trip in Mel's SUV. The diamonds had been a graduation gift from her mother. Mom and Grandma were in the habit of giving her jewelry on special occasions. They knew Lexie wouldn't spend money to buy such things for herself. She placed her musings on hold and rose from the white lacquered ladder-back with the wicker seat. It occurred to her that the dressing table and chair were probably antiques. She slipped into a pair of low-heel white pumps. Then Lexie picked up her white shoulder bag along with her favorite hunter and white checked blazer. She closed the door on her way out, and started down the hall toward the kitchen to meet Maria.

"Are you expecting cool weather?" Maria asked with mock hope and a smile that didn't ring true. She was focused on the jacket Lexie had slung over her arm. She smiled back at the other woman; there was something familiar about her, but the context eluded Lexie.

"Best to be prepared. Some people really crank up the air conditioners when the temperatures rise. How long a trip is it, Maria? It's almost ten."

"Not far. We have a few minutes to spare. Would you like something to drink?"

"Just a little water." Usually a tea drinker, she didn't think that her stomach could handle another cup of coffee.

Lexie sat down at the kitchen table once more. After thanking Maria for the cool glass of water, she tried to recall another ranch within fifteen or twenty miles of this location other than the possibility of Decker's place, but she couldn't remember much and wasn't even sure exactly where his ranch was. Maybe the ranch or farm in need of a bookkeeper was in the opposite direction of the route they had taken to arrive from Lubbock. She was beginning to fret. She knew it was never a good idea to be late for a job interview. Maria finally appeared ready to make what Lexie hoped was a short drive.

"Ready?"

Lexie bit back a retort; she was in the habit of arriving early for meetings or interviews. Maria evidently subscribed to the mañana theory. Lexie retrieved her jacket and bag and followed the other woman back to the hall toward the front entry. *Now, what?* Instead, of heading out the front door, Maria stopped at the closest door to the entrance. The door was opposite the dining room. Lexie had noticed when she arrived the day before that both rooms at the front of the house provided a pair of large windows with a view overlooking the covered porch that spanned the front of the house. She figured the match to one in the dining room must be in this room, which was situated in line with the bedrooms. Lexie was still working on controlling her volatile temper and fighting the urge to ream Maria a new one when she heard Cutter's voice.

"Come in, Lex. Have a seat, I'll be right with you."

He was seated behind a huge mahogany desk talking on the land-line. "That tears it!" She mumbled and turned around to track the retreating Maria.

Cutter set the phone down and went after her. "Lex, please come in; take a seat until I get off the phone. Then we'll deal with the interview."

"Damn it, Cutter, I'm going to be late!"

"No, you're not. You are right on time, but I am running behind."

At that bit of news she became furious, but followed him back into the room. There wasn't any job. It was only a ploy to get her out here when she refused to return to the hospital. She attempted to cool her rising temper by taking in the large, very masculine, room. A moderate sized bar that matched the dark desk was placed near the front of the room not far from where he was seated. The four wood backed-bar stools looked more modern, but the wood matched perfectly. She was making a conscious effort not to listen to his conversation, and occupied herself gazing about the room. She noted that the leather fabric on the stools matched the tanned leather of the large chair Cutter was occupying. She was failing miserably in her efforts to control her ire. Once he was finished negotiating for a hay delivery and was off the phone, she let him have it with both barrels.

"You damned lying snake! There never was a fucking job interview. Was there?"

"It's a good thing that you're a woman, Lex, if a man talked to me that way he'd be missing a few teeth."

"Well, it's damn lucky for me, then. However, if I were a man I wouldn't even be here. Would I?"

"Will you please sit down, Lex? There is an accounting job here at the Rocking R. Our bookkeeper had been with us since my father ran the place, but two months ago he retired, and I have been interviewing applicants since. I have to admit, none of them approached the interview by using foul language and calling me a lying snake. You have a unique style."

"I'm not sure I want the position, Cutter, this is the middle of nowhere. Commuting back and forth from Lubbock would be unbelievable."

"That's true, and also the reason that I haven't replaced old Bob by now. It would require the employee to live in most of the year. Maria is alone here during the day, and I haven't felt comfortable with any of the applicants so far."

"I don't think you should feel too comfortable about me around her either. I'm seriously considering kicking her butt for her part in this ruse."

"I'm not too concerned with you damaging her. You like her cooking too much."

"Her cooking is adequate, the exception being the gross sugary stuff she calls iced tea."

"Sweet tea is the norm in these parts."

"I know. It amazes me y'all aren't diabetic. Show me the books, then we can negotiate if I decide to accept the position."

Cutter sighed. That was the second time she had used 'position' instead of 'job', and he had a feeling there was a big dollar value attached to the term position. They were beginning to make headway into the bookkeeping nightmare that had been his haphazard attempt to keep the books over past couple of months. His cook gave them an excuse for a break.

Maria peeked in to announce lunch. Sliced roast beef sandwiches, Swiss cheese, and sliced vegetables for the choosing. Cutter noticed that Lexie ate sparsely and elected to drink water. Lunch out of the way, they returned to the daunting task of the books. Dinner was ready by the time they'd weeded through the mess, and she had some grasp of the ranching business.

"Okay, Cutter, assuming I agree to tackle this disorder, lets talk salary."

Cutter tried not to groan. Others had asked about how often they got paid and compensation packages, but she wanted to know about salary. He needed to take back control of the negotiation, if he even had it to begin with. "The job pays five hundred a week."

"Forget it, Cutter. I can get a position in Lubbock, Amarillo, Dallas, or Houston with a starting salary of twice that."

"Do you think you could let me finish before you interrupt me again?"

She merely nodded her head and waved her hand in an imperious way as if to say get on with it. "It's true you could probably command more in one of the large cities, but you would also have to pay rent, utilities, food, and gas for a car to commute every day. I repeat, the pay is five hundred dollars per week plus room and board. Medical insurance is usually a thirty-day waiting period most places, but we start our people immediately. If you can handle the job, you will get a hundred and fifty dollar a week raise in thirty days, and a like amount in sixty days."

"Okay, I have a couple of conditions before I accept."

Cutter was restraining the sudden urge to strangle her. "Go on."

He practically growled the last two words, but she refused to be intimidated. "One, you need to move into the twenty first century, which means purchasing a computer and appropriate software. Two, you deduct half of my salary in repayment for the hospital bills to date. Three, if you are to be my employer, absolutely no inappropriate advances. Four, I get to make my own iced tea. Five, I need to arrange to have my vehicle and the rest of my clothes delivered. Six, I have a dog."

"Is there anything else?"

"No. Well, maybe. Do you have a horse I could ride once in a while when I get stronger? I had to sell mine when I left for college."

Cutter agreed to all her terms except for the repayment of the hospital expenses, but relented when she raised a plan B. "I will apply in one of the major cities and mail a check to you each pay period."

She didn't have to worry about inappropriate advances he thought, and controlled the urge to articulate it. The more of her opinionated, nasty tempered, independent, and bad-mannered self that surfaced, the more thankful he was that they were not really married. He had known from the first day he found her cussing out the big Hereford cow that she could be a handful. He hadn't expected her to have an explosive temper, or cuss like a sailor on a bender. It also surprised him she was comfortable with horses, given her horrified expression at his suggestion she mount Rowdy on the hasty exit from the rising creek. The thought occurred to him maybe it was riding with him, and not the size of his horse that had worried her.

He retrieved a small envelope from his top desk drawer while she was filling out the required employment information, and then traded with her for the completed paper work.

"These belong to you. They were sent home with me when you were admitted to the hospital."

Lexie peeked into the envelope and found her missing diamond earrings and a silver bracelet watch still caked with mud and no longer keeping time. "Thank you. The diamonds were a graduation gift from my mother and grandmother."

Lexie never made dinner that evening. She decided on a short, pre-meal nap following a long exhausting day. She was dead to the world until nearly ten the next morning.

******

The following week Lexie'd put a serious dent into the huge backlog of the ranch bookwork caused by Bob Henson's departure. At that point in time, the Rocking R owned a powerful computer along with a printer, scanner, copier, and fax machine combination. Cutter decided his new equipment rivaled that of the corporate offices in Dallas.

A week to the day from her call to the Potters, Mel's mother phoned Lexie seeking information about her missing daughter

"I'm sorry, Mrs. Potter, but her phone continues to say she is out of the area. Could be that or it's turned off, and her phone is the only way I have of contacting her. My mom got the same kind of message when I lost mine. I also tried to reach Mel on the landline at the hotel, but someone else is occupying our old suite. The desk clerk at the hotel told me she'd checked out last week."

"We've had similar results with our inquiries. Lexie, if you hear anything please let me know. I just dropped Benson off at the airport. He's on his way down there in the company jet to bring her home. He took Booker with him."

"I'll call him as soon as I talk to Deputy Sheriff Boyd. He may have more information. Try to get some rest."

Lexie immediately called Patrick Boyd to give him a heads-up, and then gave him Benson Potter's phone number. Boyd called her back a short time later to say he was meeting Mel's dad at the airport to escort him out to the Decker place. Boyd promised to keep her advised. Then she placed a call to Mr. Potter to confirm arrival. He also agreed to keep her updated on events. It seemed that no one had been able to reach Mel. As promised, Lexie called Mrs. Potter back to apprise her of Deputy Boyd's involvement.

"The deputy is meeting the jet with a search warrant in hand. He'll also be driving Mr. Potter and Booker out to the Lazy K. It seems that your husband filed a missing persons complaint with the sheriff's department. Don't worry they're in good hands; Patrick Boyd is an extremely competent lawman."

I have really opened a can of worms. Wait until Decker gets a load of Booker, she thought.

Cutter walked in while she was reassuring Mel's mom. She set her little phone on the huge antique desk, which had once belonged to his great-grandfather, and blinked back the tears threatening to fall.

"You look like you could use a break, Lex. I have to run to the feed mill. Why don't you tag along? We can have some lunch out for a change."

"Is there a bank near where you're headed?"

"Sure, the one we use is nearby."

"Do you have time to stop so I can open an account?

"I reckon we can manage that."

She saved her entries, logged out of the computer, and hurried down the hall to the blue and green room she now considered hers. Lexie gathered photo IDs and her first paycheck, and stuffed them in her new brown shoulder bag. It wasn't leather like the old navy one that was beyond salvaging, but it served the purpose.

Cutter and Lexie headed south for the afternoon, while three determined men were heading in the opposite direction, toward the Lazy K.

CHAPTER 8

THE desolation was mind boggling, and Benson Potter could not imagine his daughter being isolated in that depressing countryside. Black-winged harbingers of death caught his attention not long after the deputy informed them they were on the Decker spread. Deputy Patrick Boyd's silent prayer echoed those of the other men at the sight, *Please Lord, not Melinda.* Patrick veered the Bronco off road toward the circling buzzards. Relief circulated as much as their prayers had that the remains they found were not human. Four young calves in various stages of decomposition rested in a dry riverbed. It was obvious they had starved to death. Their emaciated mothers stood by too weak to go on. Without feed or water, the cows' milk had dried up long ago. The small herd had probably traveled from one water hole to another in a search to quench their thirst until the young had succumbed. Holes dotted the riverbed where the thirsty cattle had pawed hoping to dig down to some moisture. Patrick took photos to document the devastation.

The mood had turned even more somber the closer they got to the house at the Lazy K. Boyd exited the sheriff's vehicle and approached the door. The place appeared deserted. No one responded to his knock or the doorbell at the front of the house. He worked his way around back to check out the rear entrance. He returned to the vehicle and drove the short distance to the equally dilapidated bunkhouse. It was obvious to the three men that maintenance had been lacking for many years. Only one grizzled old man occupied the place. Patrick questioned an old ranch hand by the name of Pete.

"Yep, I be the only one left. Rest of em' skedaddled. We ain't been paid fir more 'n five months. I'd go too, but this is home. Was hired on by Miz Sophie's husband Karl back when we was all young."

The old man identified the photo of Melinda as Decker's live-in lady friend, but he didn't have a clue as to where the couple could be. They were about to call it a day and in the midst of discussing the option to report Melinda missing to a wider network of law enforcement. Their decision was put on hold when the sought-after pair barreled into view. They arrived in a choking cloud of dust.

David noticed the marked Bronco immediately. Boyd he knew. The tall graying man he recognized from his research as Melinda's rich daddy. He possessed the dark hair and brown eyes inherited by his daughter. The powerfully built third man was a mystery to David. He pasted on his most charming smile and played the gentleman role to the hilt as he opened Melinda's car door. "Look, Sugar, we have company."

She knew all three men, but stared at them through the blank eyes of a deer caught in traffic; they were strangers to her. Benson moved forward speaking to her like he used to when she was a child and had a bad dream. Finally, she responded to the familiar voice from her past.

"Daddy? What are you doing here?"

His daughter was disoriented and confused. He made an attempt to reach her on a basic level. "Where else would I be except by your side when you need me?"

Quite unexpectedly, she launched into her father's arms sobbing like a small child.

Patrick called for a backup team to search the house. Once the deputy gained control of the rising urge to rip Decker apart, he served the warrant. Melinda didn't resemble the girl he had met a couple of weeks earlier when he'd searched for her friend, Lexie. Benson's daughter had lost an alarming amount of weight in a short period of time. Her stylish pink sundress hung like a rag from her shoulders. The lawman had to admit Decker was cool under pressure; he continued to act as if their presence was merely an unexpected social call. Patrick read him his rights, cuffed him, and stuck him in the back of the Bronco to marinate. Patrick and the others stood in what shade the covered porch provided while they waited for the rest of the team to show up. Patrick made the suggestion to Potter's paramilitary companion that he take a look at the vehicle the pair had just arrived in. As a civilian Booker wasn't bound by the warrant issue.

Benson had introduced Booker when Patrick picked them up at Preston Smith airport. Alarms went off on first sighting; Patrick had seen more of the man's ilk than he cared to remember during his tour in Iraq. Tall with a cleanly shaven head, the bodyguard's eyes were obscured by aviator sunglasses, but the deputy sensed that Booker registered every element of their surroundings. He had a couple of inches on Patrick in addition to fifty or so pounds, and a don't-mess-with-me attitude that reminded him of Cutter Ross. Booker returned with the girl's handbag along with a suggestion to extend the warrant to include all vehicles on the premises.

The Sheriff showed up before the crime scene team that his senior deputy had requested. Benson and his little girl went in the sheriff 's vehicle. Their destination was the closest clinic able to assess her condition. Before they departed Booker returned Melinda's handbag to her and conferred briefly with his employer.

David was sweltering in the back of the Bronco. Not long after Melinda and her father had driven off with the Sheriff, his gut clenched with the arrival of three newcomers who checked in with Boyd. They'd driven up in an unmarked. Once they entered his house, Boyd came to escort him into the blessedly cool confines of the living room. Still cuffed, he remained just inside the front entrance in the custody of the big bald guy. The hulk had removed his sunglasses upon entering the house and his sherry colored, cat like eyes, nailed David to the floor. He was reluctant to budge the guy looked at him as if he wanted to squash him like an annoying bug. He had news for the Terminator; he would have to stand in line. David had been able to pay back a large amount to his bookie today, thanks to Melinda's insurance settlement. That should buy him some time. He'd held back enough to purchase an engagement ring, but Melinda's dad showing up could prove to be a problem. He stared at the goon squad trashing his place and instinctively knew it was Lexie he had to thank for this turn of events.

Patrick was reluctant to turn Decker loose, but the only thing the search turned up was a revolver in the glove compartment, for which he had a permit. The remainder of firearms on the place consisted of usual arsenal found on farms and ranches. They confiscated what appeared to be over-the-counter aspirin, ibuprofen, and the like for analysis. After searching the outbuildings and the bunkhouse, there was little else to do but remove the cuffs. "Stick around, Decker. If Potter decides to file kidnapping charges, I'll be back for your sorry ass."

Booker had known Melinda for close to a decade. He was aware she struggled with relationships. "What do you think she sees in that guy?" he asked Boyd.

Patrick was wondering the same thing as he and Booker left the unproductive search, and Decker behind. Benson, keeping in touch with his bodyguard and Patrick, notified them that Melinda had been admitted to a hospital there.

Melinda underwent a Jekyll and Hyde switch the following morning. The attending physicians assured Benson her reaction was normal for an addict going through withdrawal. She needed to be restrained from ripping out the IV that was dripping fluids into her dehydrated, anorexic-looking body. The attending physician suggested to Benson that a private psychiatric hospital nearby would be able to offer better care and rehab.

Her father moved Melinda the following day. The private facility was costly with carefully restricted visitations and state of the art security. It was the best choice to keep her out of Decker's reach. It still galled Benson the law hadn't found anything that would lock Decker away. Deputy Boyd had reminded him they still didn't have the toxicology reports back on the contents of the medicine cabinet or the pills found in Melinda's purse. If the law couldn't find enough evidence to arrest or convict him, Benson would see that David Decker paid for the abuse of his daughter.

CHAPTER 9

"My God. This is outrageous!"

Cutter was enjoying a few quiet moments over his delayed lunch when he heard Lexie holler. He prayed she wasn't talking to a client. Bookings for the stallions were way down due to the economy and the damn drought. He'd even left some of his best mares open for the spring. The last thing he needed was to have her alienating a potential mare booking. She'd been in a good mood two days earlier and pleasant company. It had been the phone call from her friend's dad to inform Lex that they had found Melinda, which burst her good mood balloon. Her friend's condition and the lack of physical evidence implicating Decker set off a drastic change in her disposition. She'd been on a tear ever since, and he'd been avoiding her for just as long. He'd never lost his temper with a woman, but was approaching his breaking point with this one.

"Son of a bitch!"

He stormed across the hall to reprimand her for the use of foul language. He realized immediately his error; she wasn't on the phone, but going over recent invoices. She looked up from her work and let him have it.

"Cutter, are fucking crazy? Do you have unlimited funds that you can throw money around this way? I thought you were fairly intelligent, but I'm seriously reconsidering my original assessment."

He plunked down in his leather chair beside the desk where it had been exiled when her ordered, gray-cloth, adjustable swivel chair on rollers had arrived. "What the hell offence have I committed this time?"

Lexie noted that he seemed pissed and was growling like a bear, but she was too aggravated to care. "Look at these invoices!"

He took the wad of offensive billings, which she'd thrust at him and glanced through the last half dozen hay deliveries. "I've already seen these. Who do you think signed the damn checks? You think these are bad, wait until the delivery tomorrow morning."

He got up and stalked out of the room. As soon as he exited, she began making phone calls back home.

The delivery the following morning was late, and Cutter had left in a foul temper, giving instructions to Maria and Sam to call him when the truck arrived. Lexie knew things worked on a schedule around the ranch. The delivery that had been guaranteed before eight that morning showed up mere minutes before noon. The driver backed the flat bed semi near the hay storage barn; it was obvious he'd made prior trips to the ranch.

Lexie moseyed out toward the barns when Sam Becker, the horse operation manager, appeared to be having a confrontation with the driver. Sam was in his early fifties still very fit and attractive, in a rugged sort of way. She had noticed that he possessed the physical form of a much younger man. His shoulders were broad, and his snug-fitting Wranglers set off his tight bum. The horseman walked with a confident swagger, but at the moment he was standing with his legs braced like he was ready for a fight. Two of the younger ranch hands stood near by waiting for instructions. The hay delivery driver was a big burley guy with a bad attitude. Lexie decided to intervene before violence ensued.

"Good afternoon, gentlemen. Is there a problem?"

"Damn right there is!" the driver was ranting. "This horse's rear end is refusing to unload or pay for the load. I want to see Ross."

"Well, you're looking at her. What can I do for you?"

"Are you Cutter's wife?"

"So I've been told."

"Then, you can cut me a check, or order this old goat to do it."

Lexie addressed the amused ranch hands. "Gentlemen, would you pull down one bale and open it for me?"

The young men jumped to do her bidding, but Sam only scowled at her. He threw his battered western straw head gear into the dirt in disgust. His salt and pepper hair was damp with the heat of the day as well as his rising blood pressure. His dark eyes flashed a warning her way. It was obvious that he didn't like her interference.

She walked over to the opened bale, pulled out a couple of flakes, sniffed them, and then shook them out. She turned to the driver. "Excuse me, what in hell is this supposed to be?"

"It is hay, lady. Are you new around here?"

"As a matter of fact, I am new to the Rocking R, but I do know hay. If this stuff was ever even decent hay, it was several years ago. I'll pay you for the bale we opened, but you can take the rest of it with you."

"I can't do that, lady."

"Well, I suggest you get on your cell or your radio and tell whoever can make a decision that this operation can't feed this crap to its horses and it will probably put the cattle at risk too. No way are we paying fifteen dollars a bale for this load. Four dollars per bale tops and the delivery charge stated on this invoice, or you can take it down the road. I've already arranged for a delivery of good horse hay at half the price."

Sam was grinning at her when Cutter and Jim arrived in a cloud of dust. Cutter demanded to know why the hay was sitting on the truck and not being unloaded. Sam directed him to Lexie.

"What's going on, Lex?"

"Negotiations. Before you start growling at me take a look at that open bale, and then tell me if you really want to pay fifteen dollars a bale for that."

She watched Cutter sift through the downed bale, much as she had done earlier. Then he approached the driver who was sitting in the cab of his truck busy writing a new invoice. "What the hell is going on? You are four hours late and my help is standing around killing time!"

"Talk to your horse handler and your wife. She refused to pay for the load."

Cutter looked over his shoulder at her to raise one dark brow in a silent question regarding the driver's reference to her as his wife. She grinned and shrugged her shoulders in reply. The driver approached Cutter. "You're a business man, Mr. Ross, not an emotional little girl. This is the best I could negotiate for you."

Cutter reviewed the new invoice, and then motioned Lexie over to look at it. He thought she'd negotiated a pretty good deal. The dealer reduced the price per bale by nine dollars. "Is this satisfactory with you, Lex?"

She shook her head in the negative, so Cutter placed the invoice in her outstretched palm. He tipped his straw hat brim. "This one's all yours Lex." He had the pleasure of hearing the driver groan.

She rounded on the hapless man. Lex waved the invoice in his face, "What are you trying to pull?" She retrieved her beat-up old wallet from the back pocket of her jeans counted out a five singles and a ten, and then handed the bills to the driver. "This is payment for the bale we opened. Take the rest of the load with you; we're finished here."

"Wait a damn minute! I told you, lady, I couldn't haul this load all the way back to Nebraska."

"I heard what you told me, but you obviously didn't hear, or believe me when I told you I could have good quality horse hay delivered for a fraction of the cost of this dry musty stuff that isn't even fit for cows. I gave you the price we are willing to pay. You haven't met our terms, and I repeat we are finished negotiating. Have a safe trip back."

Cutter was enjoying watching her tear a strip off someone else for a change, but he figured she might have pushed it a little too far. The driver—he thought his name was Hank— had gotten back in the cab. Cutter held his breath waiting for the engine to start. He was preparing to wave goodbye to three hundred bales of old hay that could have fed a lot of hungry cattle.

Instead of heading down the road, Hank handed Lexie a new invoice. "Okay, Mrs. Ross, can the men unload now so I can be on my way?"

"Certainly. Gentlemen, you may unload this truck." She handed the invoice to Cutter, and then turned back to the driver. "Please pass along to the dealer you work with that the Rocking R will only buy clean, mold-free, safe horse hay from now on. If you have hay that is only fit for cows, you will have to talk to my husband, but Mr. Sam Becker and I are only interested in this year's horse hay."

She turned and walked back toward the house, leaving the trucker and the rest of the men to stare at her retreating form. Cutter took note of the assessing stares and barked orders to get back to work. On her way back to her computer, Lexie informed Maria the lunch crowd would be a little late. Maria overheard some of the ruckus over the hay, and she felt the bossy little newcomer had over stepped her authority.

Sam delighted in telling Cutter the tale of what had happened prior to his arrival. Both men had a new appreciation for the Rocking R's little blonde bookkeeper.

The following morning, after filling the hay feeders, Cutter returned to have breakfast with Lexie. He found her eating a blueberry muffin and washing it down with a tall glass of orange juice. He snagged a muffin to go with his third mug of coffee. "Good morning, Lex. Are you feeling better this morning?"

"I'm feeling fine. I guess I was out in the heat of the day a little too long and I'm not used to it yet."

He handed her the invoice from the hay delivery along with fifteen dollars in cash. "One is for bookkeeping; the cash is what you paid for the busted bale. It was included in the invoice count. What were you going to do if he drove off with the load?"

"He wasn't going to drive off, and he'd already OK'd the terms I laid out before you arrived and he tried to padded it."

"How did you know he'd padded the deal?"

"Mel calls it my creepy sixth sense. It's not anything that I can explain., I would have been poking out numbers until my fingers were numb to replace the loss quickly, if I was wrong and he drove off with your cattle feed."

He reached for another muffin. "Can you really get good hay delivered for half the price?"

"I've negotiated a delivery of five hundred bale of a timothy alfalfa mix for next week at ten dollars a bale, fuel cost included."

He grinned the same way he did when he visited her in the hospital. "Horse hay?"

"The horses have to eat, too. But if you lose your cattle feed supplier because of me, we could probably get some cheaper, year-old, or rained-on hay for the cows. They have a much better digestive system than horses. I have a couple of ideas that may interest you if you can give me a couple of hours soon."

"Is after dinner soon enough?" She was a constant surprise. He never would have thought she had any knowledge of hay, or knew the difference between the digestive system of cows and horses.

She merely nodded to his after dinner suggestion while she watched him pick up two more muffins on his way out

Lexie entered the previous day's hay invoice a couple of hours later. She was up to date from the time Cutter had taken over the bookkeeping and payroll duties. Her next chore was to convert the past ten years of transactions from the books of Bob Henson to the computer program. She figured the task should be easier. The neat accounting style should go quicker than her employer's hastily scribbled notations had been. Lexie decided to begin work on Bob's ledgers to-morrow. She only had a couple of hours to put her research together in a methodical, cohesive presentation.

She was as prepared as she could be, considering her limited knowl-edge of Cutter's personal finances. It was stifling— another one hun-dred degree plus day. She really didn't know how Cutter and the others could work all day in the sweltering sun. She had hoped to check out the horses by now, but the excessive heat drained her en-ergy level, and she often found she needed a nap in the middle of the day.

She opted for a pre-dinner shower. Lexie really appreciated her blue-green room. Cutter had been absolutely correct when he'd first es-corted her to the room and said it was in the coolest part of the house. She made a conscious effort to conserve every precious drop of water, by cutting her usual shower time. She had come up with a plan to ensure a supply of good hay, but a magician she was not. The lack of water remained the biggest threat to both horses and cattle.

Fresh, cooling air caressed her exposed arms and legs, and her bare toes curled in the wet sand while the waves broke around her ankles. She laughed at the antics of her puppy playing tag with the gently breaking waves. The lake was calm today, but she had witnessed Lake Erie's fury sending waves over the top of the break walls, crashing to the upper reaches of giant lighthouses, and flooding out the lakeshore highways. The vision of the vast body of water disappeared to be replaced by the sounds of a gentle summer rain. It didn't last long. It left as quickly as it had come. Someone called her name, and reality crashed in; it had only been a dream.

Lexie rolled onto her back. She gazed up at the ceiling fan, which was creating the cool breeze. "Funny, I don't remember turning on the fan." She'd been thinking out loud, and nearly jumped out of her skin when he spoke.

"That's because I turned it on before I showered. Are you ready for dinner?"

"I'll be right down as soon as I change."

"You look fine. We aren't dress-for-dinner types around here."

"At least I need to brush my hair and find a pair of shoes."

It didn't appear he was in a hurry to go on ahead of her. He continued to slouch against the doorframe, in a relaxed fashion. His muscular arms were crossed over his broad chest, and Lexie was enjoying the view a little too much. *He is your employer, and you set the rules. No inappropriate advances* she reminded herself. She scooted to the edge of the bed and placed her feet on the cool floor. She could feel the intensity of his gaze as she made the short trip to the dressing table. Uncomfortable with his scrutiny, she made quick work of brushing out her hair. She banded it back into a ponytail instead of the usual more time-consuming braid. The short ankle socks she'd placed on the smooth lacquered surface before her nap were on in a flash. She stuffed her feet into a well-worn pair of running shoes. Lexie was looking forward to the arrival of the rest of her clothes. She'd packed lightly for what was supposed to be a short vacation.

She walked beside Cutter down the hall to the dining room. Breakfast and lunch were always kitchen table fare, but dinner was in the formal dining room. The fact that it was across the hall from her bookkeeping digs was convenient on the days when time got away from her. Usually, Cutter and Jim were already seated when she arrived, so she was unprepared for Cutter's Galahad routine of pulling out her chair to seat her. Her utter surprise must have been obvious; Jim was chuckling at the unfolding scene. There was an extra place setting tonight. Sam occasionally joined them for dinner, and it usually hampered her appetite. He always looked at her like she was going to sprout horns and whip out a pitchfork.

Maria was busy serving the meal. At home, everyone pitched in with setting the table, cooking meals, and cleanup after, so Lexie made the error of offering to help. She was very politely told that Maria held the job of cook and housekeeper and Lexie got paid to straighten out the books. Things were sure different around here.

Maria and her husband seemed like a mismatch to Lexie, Jim was tall, only a few inches shy of Cutter's towering six foot four, but he was slim of build. Jim's thick hair was a couple of shades lighter than his wife's raven locks, and his had a distinct auburn cast. It wasn't their physical difference—side-by-side they were a perfect ten—Jim's blue eyes radiated his good humor and overall friendly disposition.

She set her glass of tea down and listened closely to the conversation between Cutter and Sam. He had just asked his horse operation manager how his hay was holding up.

"I have enough for another ten days."

Cutter turned to Lexie. "Can we count on the delivery next week Lex or should I find backup?"

"If Mr. Williams says he'll be here, you can count on it. The timothy-alfalfa mix could be a problem, if your horses are on a radically different type of hay. Sam will probably want to transition them slowly to the new stuff."

The conversation stalled when Maria brought in a platter of one-inch thick steaks. Lexie made a conscious effort to keep from groaning out loud. She opted for the Spanish rice—a staple at the Rocking

R— some salad, and hard rolls that were an unusual treat. Maria refilled everyone's drinks before taking her seat at the table.

Cutter picked up the thread of the conversation. "Any chance of an earlier delivery?"

"I doubt it. They're still cutting some fields. Yours is already being loaded and covered with a tarp to make room for the freshly cut bales. Given the heat here, we figured already cured hay would be a safer bet. Even back home we have occasional barn fires from too tightly packed fresh hay. However, they need to cut and bail the fields before the next rain or lose it. There are a large number of clients who come and load up in the fields. Other customers take the filled hay wagons home, unload, and then return them minimizing what Williams needs to store. That will be the last of the first cutting, and it will give them some time before they have to cut again."

Jim whistled between his teeth. "How many cuttings do those hay farmers up in Yankee Land get?"

"I only know about our area. In a good year three cuttings during the growing season, but a bad year maybe two."

Between all the Q and A's, she'd been working on her plate. She'd been transported to heaven. "Maria, the rolls are wonderful! Did you make them?"

"No *Señorita*, it's too hot to bake. I bought them at a new bakery in Lubbock this morning."

"Thank you! I just experienced my second trip back home today."

Cutter decided to see what all the fuss was about; they looked like any hard roll that would be served at a fine restaurant. "She's right, Maria. These are great." He took another bite and smiled at Maria in appreciation. The rolls are almost as good as the blueberry muffins you made before you went to town."

"I didn't make any muffins, Cutter. You are in the hot sun too much."

Lexie made an attempt look innocent, and she picked up the hay discussion. Maria was already eying her suspiciously. "Sam, would you show me what forage you're currently feeding? We may not have a problem at all."

"Sure, right after dessert."

Lexie looked for direction from Cutter. The hay excursion would delay their scheduled meeting. He nodded his approval, speared another steak, and buttered one more roll. The man sure could eat. The decision to wait for Williams to arrive was made. The forage was a reasonably fresh timothy and orchard grass import, so the transition should go smoothly.

Their scheduled meeting convened approximately an hour late and didn't begin the way she'd anticipated. The first question out of his mouth had zero to do with the scheduled agenda.

"Why didn't you tell me you made the muffins?"

"I had no idea that you were going to blab about it, or I would have told you. I didn't at the time because you looked like you were enjoying them and I didn't want to ruin your appetite. You've been avoiding me like I had the plague or something. I figured you weren't likely to welcome the information. Can we get down to the reason for this little get-together?"

He moved his large chair from the front side of the desk, placing it near to where she was seated. His close proximity was distracting and causing physical stirrings she was finding hard to squelch.

"I think this would go a lot smoother if you were seated on the opposite side of the desk."

"This is fine. Proceed."

She tried to get her raging hormones under control and put her business persona back in place. "Mr. Williams and his sons will continue to supply the Rocking R with hay, foregoing sales to hay dealers, if you are happy with the quality of his hay."

"Why is he willing to haul it so far at that kind of price?"

"He's suffering with the economy like everyone else. A large part of his hay market is dependent on backyard horse owners who are now selling or giving away their animals. Unlike here, horses can graze on good pasture for five to six months, but come winter, hay—and usually grain too—is a must. If the operation is only a couple of acres, then the purchased feed and bedding can get expensive. In addition to losing a portion of his local market, he is losing part of his leased land. Family farmers and city farmers who lease out land are either being foreclosed on or selling out.

Those trying to stay afloat are planting other more profitable crops."

"How long can he supply us with hay?"

"He estimates a full year if you can handle it. Otherwise, he'll have to sell much of it to hay dealers. He'll guarantee the price for this season unless there is a huge jump in fuel prices. He's hoping to purchase some of the acreage he has been leasing if his profits are substantial enough."

"Give Williams a call. Invite him to stop over here for a day. If his hay is as good as you say, I'll put up another hay storage barn and take whatever he can sell me."

"Okay, I'll call him when we finish here. He should be in by then. I don't know how to put this delicately, so here goes. Can the Rocking R budget hold up to this? I noticed occasional transfers marked as personal funds, and more of those transfers within the last year."

"Exactly what are you getting at, Lex?'

"Normally, I don't ask questions about an employer's net worth."

"But in my case you are willing to make an exception?"

"Look, Cutter, I'm not interested in whether or not you're a cowboy millionaire—well, I am, but not for the reason you think—some of the biggest jerks I know are filthy rich." He was scowling at her and his gray eyes had lost their humor and turned to ice. "Hear me out before you decide I'm some kind of a gold-digger."

He didn't say a word, but moved his chair to the front of the desk as she had requested earlier, assessed her with his cold gaze, and in an equally cold voice ordered her to proceed.

"Okay, we'll deal in the hypothetical. If you can, without restricting cash flow, afford to invest in land, we can have an unlimited source of hay. The Rocking R, or you could buy up some of the land that Williams is in danger of losing and lease it back to him, or share crop it out."

"Do you expect me to buy land sight unseen?"

"That would make you the biggest idiot in Texas. Forget it, Cutter. I've spent enough time on this today. We're finished here. You can leave now. I'll call Mr. Williams and extend your layover invitation. Then I'm out of here."

His temper was straining at frayed tethers; the little witch all but called him stupid, and abruptly ended the conversation. "Did you just dismiss me, Miss Parker?"

"Damn right, Mr. Ross. You can stay, leave, fire me now, or let me finish up inputting Mr. Henson's books."

"How about a glass of tea? Maybe it will cool you off. Personally, I need something stronger."

Lexie watched him exit the room. She made an effort to regain her composure, and then connected with Williams. Bill Jr. answered.

Cutter was on his way back in to the office when he overheard her tell someone there was no longer a need to bother her mom with gathering her things, or to convince someone named Skip that he wanted to make the long trip. She told the person on the other end of the conversation that she had finished with the job here and would be returning home with them. When he heard her end of the discussion he entered and handed her a tall cool glass. He then proceeded to the bar, poured a couple of fingers of a much stronger brew in a tumbler, and then returned to settle into the chair opposite her. She wrote down a couple of numbers on a Post-it.

"Here are Bill Williams Sr.'s home and cell numbers. I spoke with Bill Jr. and extended your invitation. His dad wasn't at home. I left your cell number with him. The rest is up to you. I will be working on the books until they arrive. I'll show you how to operate the bookkeeping program, if you can tear yourself away from your other demands long enough,"

"Are you planning on going somewhere?"

"Yes."

That was as far as she got before the landline rang, and she handed off the call to him. Lexie had departed for the other end of the house, by the time he finished with his previous hay dealer. Neither of them was in a frame of mind to negotiate tonight. He would give them both time to cool off, and made the decision to let the subject go until morning. They had a contract that he intended to hold her to.

CHAPTER 10

Lexie's morning didn't start any better than the previous night had ended. She was in a foul mood following a fitful night where sleep eluded her. Maria shoved a congealed plate of slop in front of the blonde bookkeeper while sarcastically apologizing for not having time to make muffins that morning. Lexie was not in a frame of mind to ignore the other woman's snide remarks. She slid her chair back from the table, made a large glass of tea, and told Maria where she could stick her breakfast. A cool drink in hand she closeted her rising temper behind the office doors.

Maria viewed the way the little bookkeeper talked to Cutter as downright disrespectful. Cutter owned the ranch and was the girl's employer. He obviously was so infatuated with his little foundling that he couldn't see past her pretty face. Maria decided to make things unpleasant for the younger woman. Perhaps the troublesome blonde would pack up and go back to where she had come from.

A rising number of entries in Bob's ledgers didn't make sense to Lexie, but she ignored what appeared to be a little book cooking and copied the figures as entered. She would not question anything around here again. Hopefully, she could tough it out for another six days. Lunchtime had slipped by while she was focused on the job at hand. Later that afternoon she was distracted by the musical tones of her phone. *Great!* The call was from Mel's father with a dinner offer, and he was sending Booker to pick her up at six. The remainder of her day brightened. She looked forward to dinner with people who actually liked her and didn't think she was after their money. She remained at the computer another hour before backing up her work and calling it a day. She went to freshen up, apply a little makeup, and change in to her hunter outfit.

Ten to six she exited onto the front porch. Lexie had successfully avoided those in the dining room, or so she thought. Booker was punctual as usual, but she ran smack into Cutter and Sam on their way to the house for the evening meal. Booker exited the big rented Lincoln and came around to open the passenger door for her. "Nice to see you, Lexie. You look great! I'd heard that you'd been ill."

She gave him a friendly peck on the cheek. "It's good to see you too, Booker." She couldn't escape making the inevitable introductions. Her boss didn't ask, and she didn't explain where she was going.

Cutter didn't like it one bit that Lexie was out with Booker, or anyone for that matter. Booker looked lethal to him, but Lex acted as if the man were an old friend. It had been Cutter's intention to smooth over his knee-jerk response to her question about his wealth the prior evening. What wore on him was the way she had merely introduced him to the other man as her employer while using his surname. Technically, that was exactly what he was and he wondered why the fact bothered him.

He heard her arrive a little after two in the morning. It wasn't until she was back in her room that he was able to relax enough to find sleep.

Lexie was too wired to sleep; she got up and made a fresh container of iced tea for later in the day. She sat at the kitchen table, in the dark, waiting for the tea to steep and cool enough to put in the fridge while she mentally replayed her evening. Booker had driven to a private rehab hospital to pick up Mr. Potter who was at his daughter's bedside. Mel was much better, according to her father. She looked like the zombies in those awful sci-fi movies on late night TV, but Lexie kept that information behind closed lips.

"Lexie, is that you?" Mel asked. Her voice had sounded raspy and barely above a whisper.

"Yes, Mel, it's me."

"Where have you been?"

Obviously, Mel hadn't remembered throwing her out in favor of David Decker. "I've been ill too, but I was confined to a hospital in Amarillo. I only got out a short time ago, and came by to see you as soon as I was able."

Then, like switching off a light, Melinda closed her eyes and dismissed everyone. Dinner turned out to be a somber affair. Mel's dad updated Lexie on the investigation and his daughter's condition.

Back in the dark kitchen, Lexie moved from the table, poured the tea into a clean pitcher, dumped the tea bags in the trash, cleaned the pan, and put it away. She padded down the hall, her bare feet silently soaking in the cool floor, and then collapsed across the bed. She didn't wake until nearly ten.

Showered and dressed in a pair of cut-offs and her blue hospital gift shop tee, she made her way to the kitchen for a glass of orange juice. Luck was with her and Maria was not in the kitchen to throw more visual daggers at her.

Juice in one hand, and two slices of heaven tucked under her arm, she went to work. She removed the apple strudel from its bakery bag, once she reached the desk. The pastry and orange juice hit the spot. Her work for the day went more smoothly than usual. Lexie got a lot accomplished.

She worked through lunch, due to her late start on the day, but called it quits a few hours before dinner.

Once back in her room, she intended to hand wash the only remaining dress slacks and blazer she had with her. She swore that she'd left them and the white tank top along with her good lingerie on the chair next to the bed. Not able to find them, she reluctantly went to check with Maria. Oh, sure! Maria was only being helpful. Lexie knew the housekeeper had deliberately washed the cottons on hot, and dried them on high for good measure—three hundred dollars worth of her best clothes had shrunk to toddler size. The hunter slacks had run all over the white tank, as well as her bra and panties. The beautifully form fitting checked blazer had shrunk around its lining and resembled a tie dye of various shades of green. Lexie restrained her temper as she carried her trashed garments back to her room. "Only five more days," she told herself.

Cutter made a point to escort her to the dining room that evening. He requested a brief meeting following dinner. Lexie agreed, thinking she needed to show him how the new bookkeeping system worked.

Maria brought in the food. She was all sweetness and innocence. Lexie wanted to smack the smile off her face. Only Maria's husband, Jim, noticed the tension between the two women. He also knew his wife was up to no good.

Sam and Cutter were busy discussing horses and were oblivious to the emotional strain of the two adversaries. Lexie started mentally counting the remaining days; if she made it through today, there were only four more. She picked up her tea, took a big gulp, and gagged on it. She got up so fast that she knocked her chair over, and then stormed into the kitchen to confront the cook. "Maria, you gave me the wrong tea."

"I'm sorry Señorita, but we only have one kind of tea in this house."

Lexie went to the fridge to locate the unsweetened tea. "Where is it? I made a fresh pot early this morning."

Maria smirked, like someone who knew they had seniority and the upper hand. "Oh, you mean the drain cleaner?"

Lexie quietly returned to the dining room. Maria was feeling triumphant.

At the dining table, Lexie retrieved the offending glass of liquid and returned to the kitchen, where she threw the contents into the other woman's face before pitching the glass into the sink. The men heard Maria scream, followed by a loud shattering sound.

"What's going on in here?" Cutter sounded upset.

Too bad; so was she. Maria claimed that Lexie attacked her, which was technically true.

"What about it, Lex?" Her employer asked.

"She's lucky I only gave her a bath in her diabetic brew. Oh, by the way, I quit."

"You can't quit. We have a deal."

"Well, she broke the deal, and then some. I stayed up until three thirty this morning so I could brew tea for today, put the container in the fridge, and cleaned up. Your sweet precious Maria threw it down the drain." At that point, Lexie turned to confront the cook and informed her, "You win. I'm out of here. One more thing, Maria, I was never any threat to you. If I'd wanted to cook, clean house, and cater to some man's whims I wouldn't have spent years of my life getting a college degree."

She turned her back on the occupants in the kitchen and headed toward the rear of the house to pack her few remaining personal items.

Cutter made the trip down the hall with all the enthusiasm of a condemned man walking his last mile. What could he say to her? She was packing her luggage. The tears running freely down her face undid him. Since he first found her cussing out Mamma cow, he'd never seen her shed a tear. It appeared the dam had burst. He wrapped her in his arms while she soaked the front of his chambray shirt.

"Come on, Lex. Isn't this a lot of fuss over a pot of tea? Maria is making a fresh batch for you."

She shoved him away, picked up the damaged clothes, and then threw them at his feet. "I only had two good set of clothes with me. My navy suit was trashed rolling in the mud when I had the misfortune to happen onto the Rocking R. Today, Maria deliberately ruined this outfit. It might not mean anything to you, but I paid over three hundred for this pile of rags that I only wore a few times."

"May I come in?"

Doctor Callahan was standing in the doorway.

"Sure, Doc, come in. I have a couple of things to take care of, so I'll leave you two alone. Lex, may I have these?"

She gazed down at the shrunken mess still at his feet. "Throw them in the trash, or burn them. It doesn't matter to me."

Once the doctor was finished examining the girl, he went down to the kitchen to locate Cutter. From his patient's accounting of the shenanigans taking place around here, he was pretty confident that he would find the boss there. He overheard Cutter telling Maria she would have the cost of the ruined clothing deducted from her pay. Maria was warned that should anything like this happen again, she would be fired.

"Cutter, she attacked me!"

It was obvious that Cutter was losing patience with her, so Joe interceded. "I don't think Lexie attacked you, Maria. If she had, you likely wouldn't be standing and would probably need my services more than she does. Could I bum a cup of coffee?" Over coffee and a slice of strawberry pie, Doc Callahan discussed Lexie with Cutter.

"Physically she's doing better than I expected. It's her emotional state that concerns me. You are as much to blame as Maria for her agitated state."

"How do you figure that?"

"Didn't you accuse her of being a gold digger?"

He didn't say a word, but just stared at the older man.

"You know, Cutter, she could have really hurt Maria if she'd lost her self-control."

"Doc, do you call drenching a person in tea and throwing the empty glass across the kitchen self-control?"

"Since she's a first level black belt, I would say she had a lot of control given the situation. I left her a couple of sedatives. She needs a good night of sleep, and I want to see her tomorrow afternoon."

Lexie finished her packing while she continued to be the topic of conversation at the other end of the house. Once the doctor vacated her room, she called Mel's dad to ask for a ride to the rental car dealer. He agreed to send Booker to pick her up in the morning, after she explained the situation. She made her way back to the kitchen for a tall glass of water to wash down the pills Dr. Callahan had given her. She'd not expected him to still be there. He and Cutter were seated at the kitchen table working on pie. She decided to ignore them and fill the glass.

Maria knew she had overstepped and tried to make amends. "I've have made you a pot of plain tea, *Señorita.*"

Lexie went over to peer into the warm pot still on the back burner of the stove; she took a one-pound box of sugar from the cupboard and dumped the entire contents into the pot. Then she picked up the glass of water exiting the room without a word to anyone.

Callahan broke out in a ruckus belly laugh. Maria scowled at him, and Cutter was clearly aggravated.

"You think that was funny, Joe?"

"I think it was great! The fact that she struck back should go a long way toward reducing her stress."

The pills Doc had left for her must have been potent. Cutter checked on her not thirty minutes after her last appearance on the kitchen battlefield. She was out like the proverbial light. He checked on her again before he left pre-dawn to fill hay feeders and monitor the water level of the rain barrels that were set up to pump water into water troughs near the hay stations. The rain catchers positioned around the horse barn, the bunkhouse, and near the house were less than half full. Even the cisterns were straining to produce adequate pressure. Shipping water in wasn't an easy task, and cost an arm and a leg. That was part of his harsh reaction to Maria's vindictiveness. The wasting of water to purposely ruin Lexie's clothing and dumping her tea down the drain affected all of them.

Jim brought up the subject of his wife's uncharacteristic behavior. "Maria is used to being the queen bee. Another woman invading her territory was bound to have repercussions."

"She pitched right in and took care of her the evening I brought Lexie home. Your wife even called Doc Callahan. Why the about-face?"

"She wasn't happy about the Mrs. Ross deal," Jim said, "and then when you showed up with Lexie in tow again to install her as your new bookkeeper, Maria began to reassess the situation. Having two women in the same house, well, what more can I say?"

"I'll try to smooth things over with Lexie. We can have lunch out before making the trip over to see the doctor. Jim, you need to have a serious discussion with Maria. Her recent behavior will not be tolerated if I ever decide to marry."

"Are you thinking along those lines, Cutter?"

"Could be."

******

Lexie carted her luggage out to the porch, and then returned to her room to make one last sweep. She picked up her handbag and her laptop before closing the door behind her. She made the long walk down the hall, and then closed the door on that chapter of her life. She breathed a huge sigh of relief when Booker arrived in the same long sleek black car. Her belongings loaded in the trunk, and securely belted in the passenger seat she said goodbye to the Rocking R. As she stared blankly at the parched landscape she began to envision the green rolling hills, the sparkling rivers, and the vast waters of Lake Erie. Ohio beckoned to her wounded soul.

Booker hadn't chauffeured her to the rental car dealer, but to Lubbock's rendition of an International Airport. Mel's dad had refused to let her make the long drive back home alone. Instead, he'd booked a first class ticket for her to Hopkins. She would have a short layover to catch a connecting flight home, but she didn't mind a delay once she was well out of Texas. Mrs. Potter was to meet her in Cleveland.

Once she was safely in the air, tears flowed like the much prayed-for rain in this part of the country. Waves of heat rose from the tarmac as the small commuter plane took to the sky and circled the airport to head east. Lexie gazed through her veil of tears at the scarred and desolate view beneath her. The largest scars on the land below looked to be natural riverbeds, now bone dry, and the larger indents could have been man made quarries, but they were now barely discernible mud puddles.

******

Cutter returned earlier than usual to clean up and escort Lexie to lunch. He stopped by the office, but the room was empty. Concerned that she was not feeling well, he checked her room. The door was closed, so he knocked. The door handle dared him to touch it with all the threat of a hot branding iron. He already knew she was gone before he worked up the nerve to enter the room. All that remained was the scent of her. She'd exited his life as quickly as she had unexpectedly entered it.

He once again experienced the loss of someone significant in his life, but unlike the others she had only walked away. Cutter weighed his options: First, he had to track her down. That was going to be the easier task, but convincing her to return was going to be a lot more of a challenge.

CHAPTER 11

LEXIE was the furthest being from the status of a frequent flyer. She made a concerted effort to avoid the hassle of baggage security scans, long lines, personal groping, and invasion of individual privacy that were part of airline travel since nine eleven. She managed to shake off the sadness and bizarre feeling of loss that had assailed her upon her departure from Lubbock International. The four-hour layover to catch a connecting flight to Cleveland helped to push the Panhandle and a certain tall Texan to the back of her mind.

She began to relax and breathe normally as the jet's circling pattern took her out over the waters of the lake. Tension flowed from her like a heavy oppressive weight was slowly being lifted from her shoulders. The Cleveland skyline appeared pristine from the altitude the plane provided. She knew it was merely an illusion, or perhaps the city was wearing its best face to welcome her home. Finally, the giant metal bird touched down and taxied to the gate. Once on the ground, she retrieved her phone to alert Mrs. Potter. Mel's mom was already at a waiting area near the baggage claim. She greeted Lexie with warmth and a fierce hug.

"Thank you so much for alerting us to Melinda's condition. Her doctors have told us that she would not likely have survived another week."

On the ride to North Olmsted, Lexie found out more about the dire physical condition of her friend. Mel had miscarried a child! However, Mrs. Potter was more concerned with Mel's mounting depression that seemed to be delaying her return home. Mel's miscarriage must have happened after Lexie left Texas, or maybe just before. Booker and Mr. Potter may have withheld the information thinking she would have refused to leave Mel at such a critical time. Lexie had thought her friend was improving.

Neither Lexie's mother nor her grandmother was home when she arrived that evening. Skip was the only one there to greet her when she stepped through the front door of the little Cape Cod. After a lot of tail wagging and rolling on the floor, Skip made a beeline for the back door. Lexie let him out to take care of an obviously full bladder. She carted her single piece of luggage and the carryon up to her room while her dog was out in the backyard. She had called and left a message on her mom's cell when Booker deposited her at the airport instead of a rental car agency. Everything had happened so fast she hadn't been able to give them much warning that she was on her way home.

A week later, she had a temporary bookkeeping job filling in for an employee out on maternity leave. Lexie's strength was returning, aided by long walks with her German shepherd companion. She even managed a ride on her distant cousin's horse on a recent weekend trip to the Lake County home of Grandma's childhood. Gram's father was still active in the daily operations of the lakefront home and dog breeding operation. Great Grandpa Huffman had given Skip to her nearly six years earlier. Skip was only five months old at the time. It was unusual for Grandpa to have a puppy much past weaning unless it was destined for the show ring.

"This pup will be too large for breed standards. He has all his puppy shots and has already been neutered. I'll not sell him with papers, which is the reason he has been passed over many times." Lexie loved the puppy immediately, and Grandpa told her, "He is yours, Alexandra, if you want him."

Lexie watched Skip romp on the beach, playing tag with the incoming waves, and remembered the hours they had spent here when he was a pup and she was still in high school. His training had been a little tougher than she'd anticipated. He only understood German, so Grandma had pitched in. She was raised with the dogs that Grandpa Huffman had brought back with him from his stint with the occupying forces in Germany, following World War II. Thankfully, Skip learned her English commands also. Lexie was not fluent at that time, but she understood her grandmother's language fairly well. She learned to give the basic commands. She took him to the puppy obedience classes at the nearest dog trainer. The summer he was two, she and grandpa added guard dog training to his education.

Lexie had picked up German as her language class in college and also joined a German club that really helped her with speaking the language.

******

Things were looking up, and she was getting stronger. Mel, her father, and Booker returned nearly two weeks after Lexie had arrived home. Mel's return home brought threatening e-mails to Lexie's in box. She and Booker had a lunch date the week following their return.

"Do you have any idea why Mel would be sending me threatening e-mails?"

"What makes you think Melinda is sending them?'

"It was sent from her laptop. Who else could it be?"

"Her laptop and her blackberry were missing from what we were able to find of her belongings. Most likely Decker had them stashed somewhere to isolate Melinda."

"You think David Decker is sending me those messages?"

"It's probable, Lexie. Forward them to me, and I'll see what we can do. Could be the police will be able to make a connection or track the computer."

"Booker, do you think he would come here?"

"I doubt it. He's trying to spook you. He blames you for disrupting his plans, and he can't reach Melinda, so he's focusing on you."

The next few messages were more graphic in detail, as David laid out his plans when he got his hands on her. Okay, now she was spooked! Lexie signed up for more martial arts sessions. She was rusty and out of shape. The lessons boosted her confidence and her strength. She doubted that she was strong enough to take on someone like Booker, but she could defend herself against David if it became necessary. She had begun to jog part of her evening outings with Skip. None of her physical workouts, the addition of CPA online classes, or her temp job kept the nightmares at bay.

Once again in her dreams, she was transported back to the drought-stricken place she had recently escaped. It was the image of a tall dark cowboy on a coal-black horse that was adding to her insomnia whenever David's menacing countenance wasn't disrupting her sleep. Cutter was searching for a stray and he had picked up the trail. She shivered and pulled the quilt tighter around her.

Mom had begun questioning her mounting sleepless nights. Lexie figured she must have called out in the grips of one of her nightmares.

She hoped it was only the late night baking sprees when she couldn't sleep that had set her mother on the forty-question routine. Lexie couldn't tell her much. Booker had warned her to keep the Decker thing under wraps until he could get a handle on it.

"The last thing that we need is for Melinda to get wind of this, and think that Decker is still a threat to her."

Lexie agreed with Booker's assessment, so she kept silent about what was tormenting her sleep.

As much as she loved her mom and grandmother, neither of them could keep a secret. Lexie wondered if her ability to keep a confidence was a trait inherited from the father she never knew.

CHAPTER 12

Benson thought Lexie had the right idea; it was time to get out of Lubbock. Nearly two weeks had gone by since their return, and nada from the lab results on the impounded medications. Decker may have escaped the clutches of the law, but retribution for what he had put his daughter through was already in the works.

Cutter had struck out in his efforts to track down Lexie in the days immediately following her disappearance. Not one of the rental car agencies had a record of her or someone of her description renting a vehicle. Reluctantly, he contacted Patrick Boyd. The lawman wasn't as cooperative as Cutter had hoped, but he was able to find out Lexie had flown home. His myriad of questions went unanswered behind the guise of an ongoing investigation. He was stymied for the moment, but was hopeful that the Williams boys could shed some light on his elusive prey. Her destination was obvious, and her employment records listed her address. However, it was the feel for her history and how it shaped her eclectic personality that interested him.

The hay delivery went off without a hitch, and the quality of the hay was even better than he'd hoped for. No wonder Lexie had wondered about his intelligence, considering the outrageous price of the last load. The hay dealers knew they had the upper hand. The longer the drought lasted, the worse it was going to get. Pay the price or let your stock starve. Cutter hashed out a deal with Williams to buy as much hay as he could supply. Consequently, he had to put finding his missing bookkeeper on hold while he and a handful of his crew got to work on a new hay storage building.

******

Cutter's neighbor at the Lazy K was bemoaning the loss of his golden goose. Melinda's father had spirited her directly home from the secure psychiatric facility, effectively putting her out of his reach. Funds from the insurance settlement for her Caddy had bought him some time, but not much. His gambling debts were likely to have the buzzards picking his bones sooner than later. At present, his best option, it appeared, was to lay low while he figured out what assets he had left that would generate cash.

The universe continued to crap on him. Now the local media wanted comments on the story that appeared on one of the national TV news broadcasts featuring the starvation and loss of cattle due to the prolonged Texas drought. There were graphic photos taken at the Lazy K during a police investigation into the disappearance of an Ohio woman. David hadn't a clue what the reporters were ranting about. He searched the news archives on his newly acquired laptop. It had galled him that he had to buy the pricey item so that he could have an Internet connection, but the sheriff's people had confiscated his PC, so he didn't have much choice. He only used Melinda's laptop to put a scare in to Lexie Buttinski.

The news footage had turned his stomach, and a sudden cramping sensation in his midsection sent him to the can. "How in the hell am I going to maintain a low profile with my home splattered all over the

TV?" He grumbled after rinsing his mouth out with a shot of booze. He speculated on where the media had obtained the material they used for their story. Did Boyd release those photos, or was this attack coming from Melinda's well-heeled father? Whichever, he decided his troubles were a direct result of the blonde bitch's interference.

The end of July brought record temperatures without any signs of relief. More carcasses decorated the Lazy K, and David—hiding out from the media, and from a loan shark he'd been forced to use—had crawled into a bottle of cheap whiskey. Then fate finally took a positive turn, and his fortunes suddenly underwent a reversal. An impressive offer came in on the place from an out-of-state conglomerate. The gray haired, slightly bald, real estate agent suggested he grab the offer. The guy was as old as dirt, and his faded blue eyes felt like they were peeling away all David's secrets when he said, "Look, Mr. Decker, only an out-of-town buyer would make an offer on this place."

David wanted to make a counter-offer, but caved in when it was made clear by the buyer's attorney that this was a one-time offer, "take it or leave it." The agent reiterated the fact there wasn't a soul in this part of the country who would be interested in Lazy K. David reluctantly signed the contract, after the old man picked the scab of a slowly healing wound. "In addition to the condition of the property, all the bad press is bound to limit the small pool of buyers and significantly lower the value even more." Though the broker with the dubious title of Honest Hal claimed to have the ranch owner's best interest at heart, David wondered if it was his interest or the new owner's that old Hal was looking out for. At this point in his life, it didn't matter; he needed the money. David had paid his debts to the loan shark, packed what he deemed of value, and moved to Miami before the end of August.

******

Pete realized the Decker whelp was gone for good, leaving him to scrounge what he could for himself and the few remaining horses in his care. He swallowed his considerable pride and climbed in his old pink, once bright red, Ford pickup. The old engine fired to life, after a lot of grinding and sputtering, backfired a few times, and then roared away in what resembled a minor haboob.

Cutter and Sam kept a close eye on the growing cloud of dust making its way toward them long before the sound of the muffler-less old beater announced its approach. Old Pete from the neighboring outfit to the east alighted from the ancient truck. Cutter remembered Pete from the days when Sophie ran the Lazy K. The once slim fit man resembled an old scarecrow. Cutter wondered how long it had been since Pete had last seen a decent meal, or had a bath. At one time, the veteran cowpoke could have stood eye-to-eye with him, easily matching his six foot four. Now the old cowpuncher was bent and stooped from a hard life, as well as from advancing age.

Cutter invited Pete to lunch, and his cataract-shaded brown eyes were close to tears. Not since Sophie died had anyone invited him for a meal. Pete explained his dilemma, over lunch. "Don't know when the new owners might show up, or if they even will. Ain't been paid regular for nearly a year. I be the only hand left. Cow bones the only things growin' on the place. Mah poor remainin' hosses are starvin', but I cain't bring mahself to shoot 'em. I know things are tight everywhere, but if you could see your way to front me some hay fir mah hosses', I'd work fir you fir free."

Cutter and Jim loaded one of the ranch pickups immediately following lunch, and went down the road behind Pete to the Lazy K. The bags of bones that once had been three good cowponies made Cutter want to get his hands around Sophie's no-good grandson's neck. "You have any water left, Pete?"

"Not much, rain barrels are close to dry."

So Pete, his noisy pink truck, and the scarecrow horses joined the crew at the Rocking R.

Cutter assigned light duties around the horse barns to Pete as Sam had suggested.

The new hay barn already had several loads of what Lexie had dubbed good horse hay. Sam and Jim were capable of handling the ranch in his absence. Nearly two months after her defection, Cutter went to locate his stray bookkeeper.

Excerpt: Panhandle Mayhem

WHILE Cutter and Mr. Potter were negotiating high finances the following day, she was visiting with Melinda. Lexie was the bearer of a much larger container of baked goods this time. She also purchased two large glasses of tea, complete with accordion-necked straws at the cafeteria on her way in. A peek inside at the contents of the huge vessel sent her friend into peals of laughter.

"Wow! Are you trying to put me into a diabetic coma?" Mel inventoried the confections: oatmeal cookies, brownies, chocolate chip cookies, and macaroons. "When did you bake all of this, Lexie?"

"Last night. I couldn't sleep, thanks to a certain Texan's twisted sense of humor. All my online work was caught up, and I was too agitated to read, so that left baking. Anyhow, you don't have to eat it all at once."

Mel was intrigued; it was unusual for any man to have much of an effect on Lexie's focus. "What did he do?"

"Just as I was ready to snuggle under the quilt Gram made at her quilting bee, the one she gave me for my birthday when I turned twenty-one, he calls, and ends with *sweet dreams*. I mean he…knew damn well I wouldn't be able to sleep after that."

Mel was munching on a nut-filled brownie while contemplating what she had just heard. "That doesn't sound so bad. Why would that keep you up all night?"

Lexie merely stared at her friend, selected an oatmeal cookie, rationalizing it as the breakfast she'd skipped, and washed it down with a long drink of tea. She set her drink back on the adjustable bed table they were sharing and gave her friend a very graphic description of the scene in the drive the night before.

"I told you he was here for more than one reason. But no, you didn't want to acknowledge the hot looks cast your way. Well, Lexie, you can't hide from the truth any longer. You've found Mr. Right."

"Cut the Mr. Right crap, Mel. It wasn't anything other than pure animal magnetism. The man is loaded with it."

"So, you admit you're attracted to him."

"I don't deny that. Still, it's no excuse for losing control. Thank God that I don't have to see him, or try to avoid the prospect today. I don't think I can face him."

"Aren't the two of you going to dinner with Mom and Dad tomorrow night?"

"Don't remind me. Actually, I was thinking of taking a trip up to Kelly's Island, and keeping a large part of Lake Erie between us until he goes home."

"Come on, Lexie, you're not a coward. Are you going to let him get away? You'll regret it the rest of your life if you do."

"Mel, I know you're a hopeless romantic, but let's get real here. Cutter and I are diametrically opposed. I mean talk about opposites attracting! We would be at war constantly."

"Are you sure? The two of you looked pretty comfortable together the few times I have seen you in his company."

"All that aside, Mel, there is no way in hell that I am ever going back to Texas. I hate the place."

"You can't hate the whole state, Lexie. You only saw a small part of it during the worst drought in a century."

"Do you watch the news at all? It's not only the drought and wild-fires; drug traffickers run their poison unchecked across the border and onto private farms and ranches. They threaten the owners and their families with impunity."

"Lexie, you know we have more than our share of crime in Ohio. Instead of drought, we have flooding of rivers and creeks, but we have a lot of the same problems."

"Stop trying to rationalize things, Mel. We don't have rattlesnakes, or Maria Rodriguez."

"I know. It is kind of a role reversal. You're usually the rational one trying to keep me from over-reacting. Who, the hell, is Maria Rodriguez?"

ANOTHER PANHANDLE
MAYHEM MOMENT:

"How are you holding up, Mel?"

"Really good. The food sure beats the hell out of the hospital slop. So far, it has been very entertaining."

"I noticed you only danced once, and I know you love to dance. Is it too much for you?"

"Have you ever danced with your father?"

"No. I never knew my father, or at least not that I can remember."

"Sorry, I forgot. But dancing with my dad is not a real hoot."

"So let's shake things up a little bit. Ask Cutter to dance with you, and I will dance with Booker."

"Shake things up? You mean start a war. Cutter will go after him."

"No he won't, because you'll explain to him that Booker and I are merely old friends."

"Cutter isn't going to want to dance with me."

"Sure he is. He is a man, and you are a beautiful woman. If he should be reluctant, promise you'll tell him something about me that he doesn't know. But first go flirt with the band; find out if they have some line dance tunes in their repertoire."

Lexie returned to her seat, but Mel kept going around the edge of the dance floor. Mr. Potter was about to go after her when his wife restrained him. He directed his attention and his question to Lexie.

"Where's Melinda going?"

"To request some special tunes."

He sat back down but kept a watchful eye on his daughter. Booker hadn't taken his eyes off of Mel since they re-emerged from the ladies room. Cutter reluctantly agreed to dance with Mel, but he was less than happy about Lexie's plan to dance with Booker. As planned, on the next set of slower music she latched on to Booker and dragged him on to the dance floor, right behind Mel and Cutter. A couple of songs later, they were all back at the table while the dancers changed again. Absently, Lexie picked up her drink and downed some. She noted that Cutter had switched back to coffee.

The music stopped, and the bandleader announced a twenty-minute break. During the break, desserts were ordered

Twenty minutes flew by while she tried to explain the planned trip, in response to his question about why she would want to go out to the middle of the lake. She hoped to God that Mel hadn't told him it was to wait out his inevitable return home. That was the first thing she asked as she and Mel took to the dance floor, dragging Booker with them. Cutter declined to join them when the band announced a set requested by Melinda Potter.

"No. I didn't tell him you were thinking of turning tail; I only mentioned you were planning a trip out into the lake for a few days."

Cutter was enjoying the view. The two ex-roommates were having a good time; it was obvious that they had danced together quite a bit at the local establishments that catered to the college crowd. They hadn't stopped talking since they took the dance floor. Booker on Melinda's right would occasionally roll his eyes, or shake his head at parts of their conversation. It amazed him that the guy could be taking in their chatter, continually scan the room, and yet never miss a step.

Cutter managed one more dance before Lexie called it an evening. She used the excuse that she was worried Mel wouldn't leave until they did. He went to reclaim her jacket while she thanked his new lawyer and his lovely wife. He held the jacket while she slid her arms in. "Thank you, Cutter."

If he were Skip, he would be wagging his tail and wanting to do the trick again just to see the warmth in her eyes, to have her smile at him once more, and thank him in that soft quiet way. She gave Melinda a hug, then turned to Booker, took hold of his hand, and leaned down to whisper in his ear.

"Always, Lexie."

*****

Cutter curiosity got the better of him. "What did you say to Booker, Lex?"

Standing under the portico in front of the Country Club, waiting for the valet to retrieve the SUV, she responded through chattering teeth. "I asked him to look after Mel. God it feels like it wants to snow. It's a good thing Mom convinced me to take her fox jacket."

The valet showed up and one of the others on duty opened the passenger side for Lexie. She slipped in and cranked up the heater while Cutter took care of the dual tip. At the first stoplight, he shrugged out of his jacket, and by the second he'd removed his tie and opened his collar. Lexie started to laugh, like someone was tickling her. Cutter figured she'd had one to many drinks. "What's so funny Lex?"

"What time is it?"

"A couple of minutes past midnight."

"Aha, the witching hour when all the princesses and princes turn back into their true form."

She stroked the fox jacket, and then unhooked her seat belt so she could remove it and place it in her lap. Cutter noticed that she continued to pet it. "Lex, are you warm enough now that it's alright to turn down the heat?"

"Oh, sure."

"Put your seatbelt back on."

"I will as soon as I let them go."

"Let who go?"

"The little foxes inside this jacket. They should appear any minute."

He pulled over at the next opportunity, and took the jacket away from her. He was worried she could decide pitch it out the window. He put her jacket on the seat behind them with his before refastening her seat belt.

"Christ, Lex, you're hammered."

"Boy, don't say that in front of my grandmother. Unless you're up to a lengthy lecture on the inappropriate use of the Lord's name."

Excerpt from Cassandra: Night Shades

JD escorted Gram to the car, and she entered the Italian restaurant on his arm. Casey walked behind the pair. Gram really seemed to enjoy herself, and it was obvious she was getting a kick out of parading around on JD's arm. Heck, why not? Casey figured it had probably been a long time since Gram had such a good looking man, one who wasn't gray, pay so much attention to her.

As for the other ogling females, Casey thought that they should get a load of him in his dress blues. That sight would have folks running for the defibrillators to restore the victims' regular heartbeats. Casey decided she was in the safest spot, behind him and temporarily out of range of his piercing blue eyes. The small parade, led by the hostess, ended at a secluded corner table, which suited Casey just fine. While JD was occupied seating Gram as if he were the reincarnation of Sir Galahad, Casey positioned herself in the corner and tried to fade into the shadows of the dimly lit room.

She wished she was able to relax and enjoy the evening, but she did not trust him. She was losing the daylong battle to subdue the tormenting ache behind her eyes as well as persistent nausea. Her order of minestrone soup and salad set both of her dinner companions on her case. Nibbling on a breadstick and sipping a warm cup of tea, she ignored them and surveyed the coming and going of diners.

Soup was served, and she felt that she had made an excellent choice: it was not disagreeing with her touchy stomach. She focused on her bowl and avoided eye contact as she listened to JD banter with Gram. Still, she could feel his eyes whenever they traveled her way and lingered. Hearing her name, she raised her eyes to meet two familiar faces.

Andy and Alice greeted Casey and her grandmother, who then introduced Jimmy.

Gram insisted that the couple join them. Casey moved over to the vacant chair next to Gram, leaving two unoccupied. Andy, no fool, seated Alice next to Casey, and placed himself between JD and Alice. Casey's sense of humor kicked in at the obvious manipulation.

She was digging into the pocket on her sundress for her vibrating cell while the newcomers placed their order. Casey asked Gram if she wanted to speak with Millie.

"You know that I can't hear on those contraptions. Just ask her what she wants."

"She says that she'll pick you up at nine in the morning."

"Tell her that I will be ready." Gram waved her hand in dismissal.

Casey thought her grandmother's hearing was getting worse. In addition to her lapses in memory, and her occasional bouts of believing Casey was still a child, Gram seemed to get confused and disorientated more lately. It was worrisome to Casey that getting her grandmother to a doctor's office depended on her state of mind and mood when it was time to keep the appointment.

"Millie, she'll be ready, but there is a small snag. Gram has company from out of town. Do you have room for one more on the bus tour? Wonderful! I'll pass on the good news. Oh, don't worry, you'll like him, all the ladies do."

"Okay, Gram you're all set, and you are welcome to bring Jimmy along." A small triumphant laugh escaped before she could squelch it. She didn't look at him as she tucked her phone back into her pocket, but she could feel his blue eyes burning holes through her like two powerful lasers.

"Did you just book him a seat on a senior bus tour?" Alice whispered while covertly glancing at JD.

"Yep. Sure did," she declared, and grinned at him when Alice broke out in a fit of giggles.

Andy spoiled the whole effect by bringing up her plans for tomorrow. "I was surprised to see you here, Casey. I thought Andi told me that you were going to the dispersal? Andy hovered right around six foot and had the same black curls that so frustrated his sister. His dark eyes were always serious, and the direct opposite of his sister's mischievous twinkle in her like colored orbs. Casey always wondered what possessed their mother to call her son Andrew and then name her daughter Andrea. Both were called Andy. They all grew up together and it sometimes got confusing when Casey would call for Andi.

"I had some work to clean up. I'm driving down in the morning."

"I suppose that the two of you troublemakers will terrorize every male on the premises."

"Andy, I'm crushed. You know my heart belongs to you. When Alice gets tired of your sorry butt, I'll be waiting in the wings." Casey gave him an evil little grin and winked at him. Excusing herself, she strolled to the restroom with Alice hot on her heels.

Casey took her time, washed her hands, played with her hair, and applied fresh lip-stain while Alice fired a barrage of questions at her.

"Who is he?"

Casey gave her the spiel about JD being a friend of Gram's.

"He's gorgeous, and those intense blue eyes. Wow!"

She decided not to comment on Alice's critique, or mention the fact that he had affected her much the same way the first time that she'd met him.

"Where is he from? What does he do?" she prodded.

"I guess he is originally from Colorado, but he is in the Marine Corps and is stationed east somewhere. Now can we drop the subject?"

"Sure. Only explain to me why he keeps looking at you like you're dessert?"

"Alice, you're letting your imagination run amok. There's nothing between JD and me, nor will there ever be."

Evidently, JD and Gram had ordered dessert while Casey was playing twenty questions with Alice. A slice of cheesecake was plunked in front of her before she finished her salad. Casey whispered to Alice, "dessert," when cheesecake was served to Gram and apple cobbler à la mode was placed in front of JD. Andy's girlfriend went into another fit of giggles that earned Casey a round of scowls. She did serious damage to the cheesecake and shrugged off Gram's disapproving scowl.

ABOUT THE AUTHOR

Author Notes:

I hope you enjoyed the characters in "Fateful Waters" as much as I enjoyed creating them.

"Troubles in Love-Land Book One" is the first encounter Lexie has with Cutter Ross. Their story continues in "Panhandle Mayhem," the second installment in the series.

Watch for the release dates on additional books in the Troubles in Love-Land series on my writing blog http://jackieanton.com/ and my author website.

Please take a few moments to review this book on Smashwords.com,Barnesan and any other review sites that you have access to.

Reader's feedback helps me know if I got it right.

I love to hear from my readers and fans. Contact me at talesby-jackie@yahoo.com and while you are there sign up for my quarterly newsletter.

Thanks for choosing Fateful Waters.

Happy reading!

Author's Website:

http://talesbyjackie.com

Other Books by J. M. Anton

Panhandle Mayhem

Book Two of The Trouble in Love-Land Series

Wind River Refuge

Is the 2015 Winner of The Next Generation Book Award in the Romance Category.

This mystery/thriller is available in E-book and paperback formats.

Cassandra: Night Shades

Release date March 21, 2016

* 9 7 8 0 9 9 9 6 2 6 4 5 0 1 *